THE SM.

THE SMALL MINE

by

MENNA GALLIE

With an introduction
by
Jane Aaron

HONNO CLASSICS

Jane Aaron, Professor in English at the University of Glamorgan, is series editor of the Honno Classics, for which she has previously edited four volumes. Her latest books are *Postcolonial Wales*, ed. with Chris Williams (University of Wales Press, 2005) and *Nineteenth-Century Women's Writing in Wales: Nation, Gender and Identity* (University of Wales Press, 2007), which won the Roland Matthias Prize in 2009.

Published by Honno
'Ailsa Craig', Heol y Cawl, Dinas Powys,
South Glamorgan, Wales, CF64 4AH.

1 2 3 4 5 6 7 8 9 10

First published in England by Victor Gollancz Ltd., in 1962
First published by Honno in 2000
This edition © Honno, 2010

A catalogue record for this book is available from
the British Library.

Published with the financial support of the
Welsh Books Council.

ISBN 978-1-906784-21-8

Cover photograph © I. C. Rapoport
Cover design: Graham Preston
Printed and bound in Great Britain by
CPI Antony Rowe, Chippenham and Eastbourne

Foreword

JANE AARON

Along the hillsides above Ystradgynlais where Menna Gallie was born in 1920, and above Creunant in the neighbouring Dulais valley where she spent much of her childhood, a few small mines are still to this day in operation. A small mine, statutorily defined, gives employment to an underground labour force of normally no more than thirty miners. When British coal production was nationalized in 1947, the Coal Board deemed such mines unprofitable, and left them to be worked by any private owner who cared to take them on, under license. Although the year in which *The Small Mine* is set is not made explicit in the novel, various indicators, such as a passing reference to a gang of schoolboys playing at being Gagarin, suggest that its events are meant to be understood as taking place in the year in which the book was written, 1961, when Yury Gagarin became the first man in space. By that date, small mines are all that are left to Cilhendre, the fictional Tawe valley village in which this novel is located. Its deeper pits have all been closed, and the majority of its workforce is employed in nearby Cwmtwrch, in which a large nationalized coal mine is still in operation. Nevertheless, for all that nationalization, initially welcomed with enthusiasm in the south Wales Valleys, no longer seems to represent quite such a brave new world, to desert the Coal Board for a job in a privately-run small mine is still seen in this novel as a form of betrayal of one's community and its values.

When Joe Jenkins, the bright young hope of an ageing and ailing village population, 'does the dirty on nationalization' to work for more money in Ben Butch's small mine, his father warns him that he is taking a job with 'no proper safety precautions, no organization and no sense of working in a community and for your community.' The father's words prove prophetic: Joe is killed in the small mine, and the news of his death, as it passes from ear to ear in a chapel congregation to whom he was to have sung 'Comfort ye, my people', shatters the community. But Joe dies in the middle of the novel, not at its close; as a whole, this is the story not so much of an individual death as of a representative Valley community, and in particular its womenfolk, as they struggle to come to terms with sudden catastrophic loss.

It is a loss, however, for which the Cilhendre villagers are, in another sense, all too well prepared; they know as if by heart the rites of grief for precisely this type of loss, and the roles they must each play in relation to it. The chasm which Joe's death opens up in the their lives widens to include all their communal memories of the 'price of coal'. Yet the mood of the novel is not heavily tragic; not only is it lightened by many instances of Menna Gallie's characteristically robust humour, but also, more significantly, it is invigorated by both anger and compassion. The anger is directed not so much against the history of coal mining in south Wales, though that plays its part, as against the atavistic forces in every society which work against social progress and damage the psychological as well as economic health of the community. At the same time, the novel is compassionate in its attitude towards those characters who are thus dragged back to the dark ages by their own primitive fears and emotions or by the behaviour patterns expected of them by their community.

As a throw-back to a harsher and more primitive era, before organised labour won its fight for better working conditions; the small mine in itself is an anachronism. It functions as chief amongst the book's representations of the atavistic, and thus appropriately gives the novel its title. But, for all its apparent focus on the world of male work, this novel is also centrally concerned with exploring the ideological pressures which impede the development of women as well as men and the socially-imposed roles which distort human potential. Although Marx may have paid notoriously little attention to the manner in which the relations of production affected women, in this novel 'the tradition of the dead generations weighs like a nightmare on the minds of the living' female as well as male inhabitants of Cilhendre. Each of the three women characters most strongly affected by Joe Jenkins' death are trapped under the dead hand of past rituals and roles as well as present griefs.

Joe's mother, Flossie, is a Welsh Mam of the old breed. 'A dark, darting little woman' when we first meet her, 'bouncing with energy and long since out of patience and passion for her slow, kindly, insensitive husband,' she lives vicariously through Joe, her only child. He is 'the worshipped, centred-on, axis' of her existence and the 'pivot' of her 'unfettered regard'. She welcomes his move to the small mine because it restores to her one traditional aspect of the Valley housewife's role, that of coping with a constant home-coming tide of industrial dirt. Unlike the nationalized colliery, the small mine has installed no pit-head baths, but Flossie enjoys the energetic bustle of dealing with her son when he returns home to her black with coal. 'It's like old times, Joe, to see a collier looking like a collier, honest,' she says to him: 'Am I a bit daft, or what? – but I feel you're more of a man in your dirt, like.'

At his death, however, she is entirely defeated; 'passive and still', she allows her neighbours to take 'her world into their hands' and is swallowed up in the formulaic repetitions and rituals of grieving. Up until the moment at which news of the mining accident begins to filter through the chapel, the reader has frequently inhabited Flossie's sharp and busy consciousness, for Menna Gallie employs to good effect in this novel a stream of consciousness narration, integrated with dialogue, which rapidly shifts its focus from one character to the next. But after the loss of her son, we never enter Flossie's head again, and never again hear her say anything but her endlessly repeated formula, 'He was the apple of my eye' – to which her neighbours in an equally repetitive refrain, respond, 'That's the price of coal, see, people don't know.' She has become a living monument to the tragic history of coal mining, and the community as a whole participates in her fossilization.

Unlike his mother, Joe's official girlfriend, Cynthia Griffiths, resists the communal pressure on her to become an icon of grief. Cynthia is the character in this text who reacts most strongly against the dead hand of the past, and is most conscious of its suffocating effects. When first introduced, she appears to represent a successful combination of the modern and the traditional, having negotiated for herself a viable and fulfilling lifestyle without having to leave her natal community. Financially independent and satisfied with her job as Coal Board clerk in the Cwmtwrch colliery, assured and confident in her dealings with both her suitors and the widowed mother with whom she still lives, she shows none of the prejudices and intolerances which darken the thinking of some of her neighbours. A visiting group of German engineers work in the nationalized mine, and many of the Cilhendre villagers, including Joe himself at first, regard them with suspicion as 'Nazis', but Cynthia takes them as she finds them, and becomes their friend. But her capacity for living in the here and now unsuits her for the role she is required to play at Joe's death.

She flees peremptorily from the chapel meeting in which his death is announced. The congregation's ready – as it were acquired – responses, its quick shift from the 'Messiah' to 'Abide with me', strikes her with horror as melodramatic and sick: 'she got up and left the place, hurried, hurried out, out to the air ... She ran into the road and thumbed a lift and ran away and talked a little to the driver of the car about the weather.' But escape is not so easy; weeks later Cynthia is still doing battle against what she sees as her mother's and neighbours' attempts to force her into becoming a 'screaming sacrifice' to their anachronistic 'idea of what's proper'. She is furious with her mother for 'drawing the curtains and trying to make me wear black, like a Victorian Miss,' and tells her, 'I'm sorry, I can't play up. He's dead ... I do miss him and I'm terribly sorry for his mother ... but I'm alive, Mam, I'm going on, see.' 'Going on' remains impossible for Cynthia within the valley community in which she is so much a figure marked out by tragedy, though, and at the close of the novel she gives up the fight and leaves for a new job in England. Her lonely exit is represented as necessary but ultimately as a defeat, rather than in any sense a victory.

Lonelier far than Cynthia, however, is the third female character to be personally and painfully affected by Joe's death. In her portrayal of Sall Evans Menna Gallie explores the manner in which a double sexual standard still operated to a punitive effect against women in the Valleys' communities of the early 1960s. Sall's husband has deserted her, and she has returned to keep house for her ailing mother and her two unmarried brothers, none of whom appear to regard her with any affection. In her isolation she allows herself to be picked up and used for sex so indiscriminately that she has acquired the nickname Sall Ever Open Door, and Joe has been one of her favourite partners. But there is nothing joyous about Sall's promiscuity; it is a guilty secret which she attempts to hide under a veneer of respectability. She allows herself no pleasure in her encounters, except for the passing sense of companionship and relation it gives her and the comfort in momentarily being wanted. In order to evoke that desire, 'she knew she had to give passivity; she concentrated on passivity as other women, the loved women, concentrated on fulfillment; this was one of the disciplines of loneliness.'

Sall too, like Cynthia and Flossie, is trapped in the chapel when the news of Joe's death surfaces, but for her the horror of the moment is increased not so much by the sense of bearing the weight of the congregation's pity but, on the contrary, by her struggle to hide from others' eyes any sign of her illicit grief. She has no right to her own feelings, as she sees it and as the villagers also seem to see it. Such is the closeness of the small community that her relation with Joe is of course common knowledge, for all her attempts to be discreet, but no one offers Sall any sympathy or support. Before his funeral, she is tempted to spend ten of her sparse shillings on a bunch of rosebuds, the dewy freshness of which reminds her of Joe's young virility, but having bought them, she panics: 'What would people think? They'd guess she'd bought them because of the funeral, they'd know.' Her memorial offering to Joe and to love is finally discarded, shoved surreptitiously beneath the seat of the bus which takes her home from her shopping trip.

According to the blurb on the dustsheet of the first edition of *The Small Mine* an 'immense feeling of solidarity one with another' is of the essence of the community to which we are to be introduced in the novel. This is certainly true of the menfolk of Cilhendre: the village, as Menna Gallie represents it, is admirably capable of supporting and containing its male members, even those who can be destructive to it. Joe's death in the small mine, although not intended, is not entirely accidental; human agency is involved in it. At the opening of the novel, Ben Butch, the small mine boss, wielding the arbitrary and anachronistic personal power which the small mine system still allows him, summarily dismisses from his employment his fireman, Thomas Davies, and hires Joe instead. Because of his low brow, jutting eyebrows and the Neanderthal slouch of his stride, Thomas Davies is known in the village as Link – that is, he is the Missing Link between man and monkey. Link is also primitive in his emotional responses: 'he was a good hater'. On the Sunday afternoon on which his death takes place, Joe has been sent by Butch to work alone down the mine, in breach of National Coal Board safety regulations. Up on the hillside above, Link takes the opportunity to revenge himself on his boss by pushing a journey of full coal wagons down into the mine, without knowing that Joe is inside. Trapped, Joe is caught in the explosion he had himself set up. But when his neighbour Steve Williams discovers the truth about Joe's death, his pity for Link leads him not only to keep his knowledge to himself, but to help Link to bear the consciousness of what he has done. He does so in order to keep the community together, and to prevent Link from causing further damage out of guilt and fear of discovery.

But, as we have seen, no such depth of understanding and care is offered to the female members of the community. On the contrary, their lives are virtually made untenable by the weight of the community's pressure to fit them into the required legitimate roles, whatever their individual feelings. Menna Gallie herself never returned to live permanently in the industrial valleys, after she had first quitted them for university. In a novel such as this one, she can be said to be exploring the cost for women of those close but male-dominated communities, and representing through her female characters' stories the reasons for her own flight as well as Cynthia's. Yet she never wrote better novels than her two Cilhendre fictions, *Strike for a Kingdom* (1959), an historical novel set in 1926, and *The Small Mine*, and of the two she herself apparently thought most highly of the latter, which was her personal favourite amongst her books. As an exploration of women's lives in the mid-twentieth century industrial villages of south Wales, before the impact of the feminist movement began to make itself felt, it does not have its equal, and as such it is most appropriate that it should take its place in the Honno Classics series.

CHAPTER 1

It was time to pack in, to clock off. Joe Jenkins, on his knees in the small coal on the floor of the stall, reached for his jacket. As he moved, the beam light from his helmet chopped up the underground blackness, travelled along the rocky heading, jumped over the stumpy, steel props, slicing triangular chunks of light out of the darkness. Still kneeling, he bent his head to pull on the coat and his light short-circuited, pinpointed, on to his knees and slender, muscled, strident young thighs and on to the colours of the coal-dust all around him.

On hands and knees, he went to the mouth of the heading where the conveyor belt pulsed and snaked, bouncing the coal. His light picked motes and beams of coal-dust in the air, like the Jesus-bids-us-shine of a sunbeam. The roof was low beside the conveyor belt; he had to pull himself on his belly, trusting that spit would be the worst he'd put his hand on. Clear of the bad part, he crawled again, came face to face, nose to nose, criss-cross of lights to cross of lights, with other colliers, in other stalls, packing in, knocking off.

In the other beams his face was black, beautified, dramatised by the coal, white eye-balls bright, a flash of teeth in the coal-rimmed lips, the licked inner bottom lip wetly red, sensual, male. The others fell in behind him; the animals came in one by one, hurrah, hurrah.

The roof lifted as they turned into a main road, and, stiff and groaning, they straightened, scrambled to their feet were able to walk, to crouch, at last, in the steel propped, Roman-vaulted, pressed-on, squeezed-in tunnel. Still they went in single file, dodging the trams heavy with coal, dodging the pools of black water between the tram lines, ducking under

the steel props, watching the ground for slippery places, for
forgotten tools that would trip a man, for meaningless
lengths of muddied chain, cast away, forgotten.

They went on; the crouching mile, two, three miles to the
cage and the electric lights; the bottom, a white-washed
cavern, archlighted, vast, inhuman. Here they waited, tired,
patient, black, eight hours of coal and darkness heavy on
their shoulders and on the thin backs of their necks. The air
was thick and artificial, like food out of tins. The cage came
down, was filled, came down, filled, took up its load; the
walls went spinning by, close, slimy, shining, fast. And on
the top it was autumn.

But before the autumn and the first cigarettes came the
pit-head baths: the comfort, the soothing, of hot water
streaming away the dirt, showering some of the weariness;
rough towels, clean clothes, humanity restored, the depravity of darkness put away in the locker till tomorrow and
tomorrow.

Joe stepped out to the hospital-clean of the lamp-room, his
wide-apart blue eyes still eye-shadowed with dust, the
insides of his wide nostrils still black with coal, his thick fair
hair rubbed on end and brittle under a tweed cap, and the
bristles stiff on his unshaven, arrogant, assured face. He
seemed taller now, now that the anonymity of dirt had been
sloughed, taller, his shoulders broad; narrow-waisted and
long in the leg.

He stepped into the cold sunshine, lit a cigarette, thought
about a cup of canteen tea, rejected it even as he tossed away
the match, and walked slowly, proudly, across the windy top,
past the trucks and the winding gear, under the shadow of the
screens, past the offices and the parked cars and so to his bus-
stop with the others.

Under their feet at the stop the ground was still small coal;
behind them was the desolation of anthracite, the great,
barren tips and the swinging chain of refuse tubs high in the

air. But across the road, the low mountain remained unde-feated; not twenty yards away grew scruffy oaks and alders, flamboyant gorse and thin willows, and in the undergrowth the brambles offered the last blackberries among the silver ghosts of rose-bay willow-herb.

The red buses came, out of the low sun; the men moved forward, slow, patient, tired.

Before Flossie had had time to lift the table-cloth to shake out the tea-time crumbs, Bryn Jenkins had taken possession of the kitchen table. Seated stalwart like a king in his shirt sleeves at the head of the table, he was doing his inhaling. His head was lost in a large striped towel, electric blue, fawn and orange, and the stinging fumes of menthol filled the small, move-only-at-your-peril kitchen. From behind the towel came grunts, gasps and the voices of drains. Bryn's catarrh was fair chronic.

Having washed the dishes and tidied the grate for the evening, Flossie was impatient to shake her cloth. She was a dark, darting little woman, still trim and tight in the figure, bouncing with energy and long since out of patience and passion for her slow, kindly, insensitive husband. Her eyes were bright, birdy, Christmas-pudding coloured, her nose a button, and the curlers in her greying hair would assert their plastic discipline until that cloth had been lifted, for combing out her sausage curls was Flossie's clocking-off signal.

'There's no good left in that old steam now. Come on, boy, finish. I'm tired of waiting.'

'Half a sec, girl,' his voice came out muffled and ade-noidal, 'leave me in peace a minute.' She stood behind him and put out her tongue at the back of his head and wrinkled up her button nose, a little monkey in curlers. Joe, their son, came through the kitchen door. Joe, the worshipped, centred-on, axis, pivot of their unspoken, unverbalised, unfettered regard. Flossie caught Joe's eye, and, lifting her hand an inch's breadth from Bryn's innocent head, went through a mime of pushing him down and drowning him in his menthol. Over poor Bryn's unsuspecting head they grinned at each other.

Bryn gave a long, final Ahh, and emerged from his tent. Not even his mother would deny that Bryn was a funny-looking chap. His large pink head was bald and bumpy, his whole face flushed and dewy now, and his eyes, pale blue and inoffensive, were red-rimmed and streaming. His nose was ridiculously long and, half-way down its length, bent itself to the left, as though to be more accommodating. The strange shape of his nose probably accounted for the catarrh, the sniffles, and the snores with which he shook the house at night. Bryn's personality swung on his nose.

'There you are, you can have your old cloth now,' he said, as he wiped his face and took some deep, experimental breaths. 'Going out, then, Joe?'

'Yes, I've promised to go to the rehearsal for the singing. Promised old Fred.' Joe was remarkably unlike his parents, though he had inherited his singing voice from Bryn, who was an inveterate follower of funerals and the acknowledged leader of graveyard singing in the valley.

Flossie looked over her son with doting criticism as he stood before the low-slung mirror over the mantelpiece, bending his knees and spread-eagling his legs. He combed his thick fair hair into a careful half-quiff, his wide, thick-lashed eyes narrowed to check on the careful alignment of each careless-seeming sweep. His nose was a proper nose; Flossie had watched that nose grow with fear and trembling, wondering often, if it came to the push, what she could sell to pay for an operation on it. But it was safe now, the boy was twenty-five and it wasn't likely that his nose would change any more. The hands in which Joe held the comb and smoothed his hair in place were big, blue-scarred, shameless collier's hands; for Joe had gone underground with Bryn, in spite of his grammar-school six years and of all Flossie's attempts to make a clerk and a gent of him.

'Look here, Joe, I don't think that black shirt and white tie is quite the thing for chapel, is it? And your Italian shoes as well! Better put on a white shirt, good boy, and a nice striped tie. Have one of your father's, isn't it, Bryn?'

Joe turned from the mirror, slowly put his comb into his breast pocket, slowly turned his head towards his mother. 'Look here, Flossie Jenkins, they asked me to sing in their old gymanfa, they asked me to waste my time in their old rehearsal, O.K.? Right; if they don't want me as I am, they can do without me, see? You don't catch me dressing like a bloody deacon for old Fred the Singing, come you. On the day, all right I'll wear a white shirt. O.K.? Wipe your nose, Dad, you got some steam left on it.'

'Why don't you wipe it for him, Joe, it's nearer you than him?' Flossie had given up arguing with Joe, but Bryn was an everlasting whipping-boy. Bryn was used to her; he had acquired, over the years patience and passivity and indifference to her, masquerading as sympathy and understanding. Father and son looked across at each other over Flossie's head, two big men and a little woman.

'I'll be off then. See you later.'

'Don't be late tonight, Joe bach, you must have your sleep – up at six and all.'

'O.K. Mam, don't fuss, will you. Think I'm going to hang about in chapel till all hours? I can see me and Fred running wild and playing noughts and crosses in the hymn books and scratching our names on the backs of the seats. Don't wait up for me, though.'

Joe left the house and Flossie went upstairs to remove her curlers and to change out of her working clothes while Bryn took up the *Daily Herald* and settled himself for a noisy nap.

'Not bad, is it, this Export? Sell a lot of it Sam?'

'Aye, you can sell anything if you call it Export, mun, ever since the war, see. People think something's got to be good if it's good enough for foreigners, for export, see, Steve.' Sam Morris took his weight on the flat palms of his hands on his bar. He was a big man, gone slack with sloth and swigging; his eyes were mildly blue and his dark hair still abundant and curly as a baby boy's, but his cheeks and porcine jowls told the tale of forty years of solid drinking and counting change. 'The war did it, see.'

'Aye, the war did a lot. Makes you think, mind. Not all bad either, not down here, whatever. I'll have another half, then. What about you, Joe? What you drinking?'

'I'll try the Export, too, ta.' Joe held out a squashed cigarette packet in his huge collier's hand. 'Have one of these? Can't do more harm to your chest than the dust's done already.'

'Damn right there, boyo. Never mind, they'll blow us all to bits any minute now, so I'll enjoy my compo while I can. Wine, women and song it is, boys, wine, women and song.' Steve Williams buried his big, bulbous nose in his export ale, took a deep, life-saving draught and said, 'Ahhh, I likes a drop of drink, aye.' He put his glass tenderly down on the bar, his hands whiter and softer than Joe's, but for ever misshapen, twisted by the years before the coal-dust cemented his lungs. His cheeks were hollowed around the jut of his nose, lines like scars cut down to his lips and he grinned a bedentured, cynical look at himself. 'Women, did I say? With this old corpus? Thing of the past, boy, thing of the past. But I got my memories, see, got my lovely memories. You got more than memories, haven't you, Joe?' He winked a rolling wall-eye in Joe's direction.

Joe dropped a veiled look, copied from the pictures, over his fair wide-eyed face and braced his footballer's shoulders as if to take on the burden of his virility. He feinted a blow at Steve's head. 'Ask me no questions, I'll tell you no lies, boy.'

'Nice little piece I saw you with Saturday. Joined the regulars, have you?'

'Shaping up nice, you know, shaping up. But, like you say, "Gather ye rosebuds while ye may."' Joe's big hand reached for his glass, and the incongruity of those hands picking rosebuds hit Steve just as he was inhaling and his sudden giggle sharpened, cut into a cough that shook through his body like a pneumatic drill. He turned away and felt for a chair, given over, abandoned, to his merciless lungs. The other two looked away and talked about the weather and Sam wiped the bar over once more and ship-shaped the glasses and bottles behind him. There was a notice tacked to the top of the bar: 'If the lady who left her corsets in the lav. will ask in the kitchen she can have them back – washed. Signed E. Morris.'

Steve was drawing gulping, painful breaths when four more men came in through the swing-door of the public bar. Black in their dirt and working clothes and heavy, muddied boots, they were anachronisms in the smart, made-over, polished bar. 'Give us quick ones for the road, Sam, we won't sit down in our dirt. Four bitters, please.'

'Working late, is it, boys? Bit of overtime?'

'Aye, we had some trouble up there today. Lost the seam and we got to blow for it. That's the worst of it see; make the money all right in a small mine, till it's worked out, but we haven't got the equipment there, not worth spending the money.'

'No, no, fair enough, but they tell me you're doing well there, even if you haven't got pithead baths and a canteen.'

'All right while it lasts, and there's still plenty of coal to cut.'

'How much d'you reckon to cut a week, then?'

'Get about two hundred tons in a good week, see.'

'Good God, honest? What sort of prices does he get, then?'

'Round about four pounds the ton, they say. No screening, see.'

'Hey,' Steve had got his breath back again and was on his feet, 'don't want a clerk up there, do you? Part-time job for a has-been?'

'He does the clerking himself, Steve.'

'Him? News to me he can write, leave alone do sums.'

'Oh, he can write his name on a cheque all right, come you, and if he makes mistakes with his sums they're all on his side, boyo. Touch his pocket and you touch his heart, that one.'

'Well, I know he couldn't write his name in school, what-ever, because he was in the same class as me. Not even old Tom the Schoolin' walloped his name into him.'

'He's come on all right now, whatever. That pint was good, Sam, Sorry to come in dirty, like. We'll go off now, have a swill and be down later, p'raps. Be seeing you.'

'So long, then.'

They swung out, crowding the door, and left the bar looking empty and desolate, the smell of coal-dust and dark lingering against the smells of beer.

'Fancy old Ben Butch making all that money, though! Bloody old capitalist! But it's in the blood, mind you; his father's relatives was bought out for thousands when the Amalgamated Anthracite came in. Made a packet they did, but not much of it went old Jack Butch's way. Remember him, Joe? Ben's father, now? No, you're too young. But you remember him, Sam; his cousins used to give him their cast-offs and that, and you'd see him, mun, going down to draw the dole in one of their frock-coats and a top-hat and an old pair of mole-skin trousers, all patched and clobbed, and his working boots on, playing the gent and touching his hat to the women. He was the idlest man in Cilhendre, honest. They say he was so lazy he used to make his wife lie on top. Bone idle, aye. She had a hard time of it, and those kids did; but there's Ben now with two cars. Two, mind you.'

'They say he doesn't know how to spend his money,' Joe added, 'and he's going to send his kids to boarding-school.'

'Good God, no. They'll give it school. Chips off the old block they are, all right.'

'Have one on me now, Steve. What about you, Sam. Having anything?'

'No, thanks, Joe, not now. No offence, like, but if I start too early I won't be counting the change right later on. The missus will bring me half a pint of cold tea in a minute, for show like.'

'Well, have a fag, then.'

'Thanks.'

'Damn, I keep counting old Ben Butch's money. Can't think why I haven't heard before how much he's making there. They ought to put him on television. "What's my line?", the last pillar of the capitalist class, *myn uffern i*. Boarding-school! That's the end, that is. Makes you think, doesn't it? Me on the compo, and I used to do his homework when we was kids. I'm getting downright jealous, honest to God.'

'I wouldn't mind a job with him myself. I could do with a bit of extra cash. Be better off then under the Coal Board. You used to say nationalisation would cure all evils, didn't you, Steve, but it's made a few of its own, all right.'

'But, Joe bach, don't you understand? Nationalisation hasn't had a chance yet; the mistake was, see, promising to pay back all that money to the old owners, interest for years they're going to have. It wasn't realistic, see? The Coal Board can't start to make a profit till it's paid off all the old leaches first. Like it always was, they got to have first cut still. The best thing ever happened to the owners was nation-alisation. Most of them was finished, *kaputt,* when the Government stepped in and saved them.'

'Aye, but it was the Labour Government, mind you.'

'Look here, Joe, don't you start on the Labour Government, not to me, whatever. Things is a lot different down in these valleys now, isn't it, from what it was before 1945, when Sam by here and me was kids. Isn't that right, Sam?'

'Well, aye, of course. No money in the pubs in them days, when blokes didn't have the price of a pint from one week to the next.'

'Are you thinking of promoting yourself to Liberal, or what, Joe Jenkins?'

'Don' be daft, mun, Steve.'

'I thought you was going snobbish for a minute and turning traitor. Your old grandfather would spin in his coffin if he thought you'd do that.'

'Is it snobbish to vote Liberal, then?'

'Of course it is; middle-class Liberal is, for blokes with cars and washing machines.'

'Well, I'm saving up for a car and Mam's already got a washing machine, and you can't accuse us of being middle-class, for God's sake.'

'Aye, there you are, see, I told you things was different. All our symbols have gone to hell. It was much easier to talk sense about politics before, indeed to God. I know I've got to be mad at somebody, but who the hell is my enemy, boy?'

'Whoever drops the first bomb, Steve.'

'Don't start on that, I can't bear it, honest. The madness of it makes me so wild I want to smash something. 'S all right, Sam, I won't start on the glasses but the bloody lunacy of it, mun! The world so nice, kids and girls so pretty, prettier than I ever remember them, isn't it, Sam? and all the old lovely things we've had for hundreds of years, standing there; old castles, mun, and, oh, I don' know, harbour walls and grave-yards; all lying there, harmless and trusting, and, these bas-tards planning to blow it all up, throw it away – like that, like nothing, like my spit. God damn them!'

'They won't do, it, Steve; they'll never do it.'

'Wish I could believe you, boy, honest, but people are so bloody daft, mun, it's frightening, isn't it, though? Makes you feel so small, like. But it's no good thinking about it, I suppose; we're helpless; us ordinary chaps, we don't count no more. Not in this world.'

'Change the subject, Steve, here's the missus with my tea. If you start her off about the bomb, we'll have 'sterics here.'

Sam's wife, tidied and combed for the evening, lifted the flap of the bar. She looked more like a deacon's wife than a publican's. Her hair, thin and gone the colour of a decaying rat, was rolled into a rigid, too-high sausage above her ears, which were large and thin and gristly and of a pale cyclamen colour. But her face was yellower, long and sad, like a horse left out in the rain. Her nose was sharp and gristly like her ears, the bone standing shining and stark in the yellow skin, and her blue eyes large and unsettled. 'Good evening, gents,' she said. 'Here's your glass, Sam,' and her false teeth cracked loose at the end of her sentence. She smiled around before adjusting them with her tongue, and Joe was fascinated by the little, delicate string beads of spit that ran from the front teeth up to somewhere in the roof of her mouth, delicate as spiders' webs on an autumn morning. Her angularity, like a pair of tongs in a knitted cardigan, was the epitome of Nonconformist respectability and Joe felt her looks were a walking blasphemy of God's creation. 'Quiet tonight, gents.'

'How are you keeping, Ellen?'

'Not so bad, Steve. How's yourself?'

'Got my old chest, of course, but I can't grumble.'

'Anybody in the saloon, Ellen?'

'Not so far, Sam; early yet. Keeping nice, isn't it?' She nodded and smiled again and ducked under the bar flap, her hips working like hinges, and the bones of her behind under the jersey skirt were as stark as a corpse's. Sam watched her as indifferently as if she was somebody else's broken-down bicycle that even the rag man had refused.

'Who was she, that girl I saw you with Saturday, Joe?' Steve asked, trying to wipe out of his thoughts the sudden vision he'd had of Ellen Morris getting into bed.

'Clerk she is in Number 4 pit. They live over in Cwmtwrch; her father's dead and her mother's got a little shop in the parlour, like. Cynthia her name is, Cynthia Griffiths.'

'Oh aye, going steady, are you?' Steve filled his idle, compensated days with asking and assessing, keeping his finger on the pulse and pregnancies of the village.

'No such luck, Steve, there's others interested beside me.'

'Anybody I know?'

'One of those German engineers in Number 4. And they got money to burn as well.'

'But that bit of opposition isn't permanent, boy; they'll be packing up soon and off to go.'

'I'm not so sure; quite a few of them have married Welsh girls and settled down here.' Joe crushed up his cigarette packet and threw it with a sudden spurt of violence into the far corner of the bar. 'Damn him,' he said, 'I don't know him myself. You know them, don't you, Sam?'

'I don't know them much to speak to, only the time of day, like. Not bad chaps, mind. Speak as you find, isn't it?'

'Bit of a change in twenty years; they used to tell us the only good German was a dead one, remember, Sam? Mind you, I can't say that I take to them. There was a lot of propaganda, I know, but them concentration camps was true, all right, and they take a lot of swallowing. Somehow, when I see those blokes on the road or going to work I don't think anything like "Workers of the world unite". I don't feel they're workers like you and me. Pity, too, because workers they are, like us. For the sake of the workers' movement and that we ought to forgive and forget, but we haven't got any business to forgive, they didn't do anything to us. We can't forgive on behalf of the Jews and the gypsies, those poor buggers are beyond forgiving. Jesus, what a world. Give us another one, Sam, and give up that cold tea myth, have a proper drink. Your missus is safe in the saloon.'

'Ta, then.'

'I don't mind the Germans, Steve, I hate that kind of cock about national characteristics and that; but there is one I don't fancy, the overseer they got in Number 4. Seen him? Real Nazi type – you know, clickin' his heels and kissin' your hand and a face like a mask. They tell me he was a U-boat commander in the war, and there was no room for prisoners on a U-boat, was there?' Joe pointed two fingers at Steve and rattled his tongue like a machine-gun.

'I'll have to watch out for him, in case I offers him a drink in a moment of weakness.'

'He's been trying to do a bit of propaganda, too, saying things like: We had to work for Krupps if we wanted work, otherwise we'd have to work for the Jews. He must be a bloody fool to think he can talk crap like that in the valleys.'

'There's plenty of bloody fools in the valleys too, boy, come you.'

'Oh, well, I'll have to go. Promised to go to singing practice tonight. Got two solos for Salem gymanfa. I promised old Fred the Singing I'd be there by eight, after he's finished with the choir. Give us a packet of peppermints, Sam, in case the preacher's there; he's got a nose like a bloodhound for a drop of beer.'

'What you singing, Joe?'

'"Comfort ye", tonight. I'll have to go, look; see you later, p'raps.' He buttoned up his coat, straightened his tie in the mirror behind the bottles, gave them a brief smile, a short-cut half-wave of the hand, and pushed broad-shouldered through the swing-door.

'Decent fellow, old Joe. Pity that girl's two-timing him, though; life's much easier when the fires are dead, isn't it, Sam? Easier, but not so nice. Give me the fires, any day.'

'I don't think young Joe goes short on his greens, though, Steve.'

'Well, good luck to him, then!'

Joe left the Red Lion in the last of the light, with darkness already gathering among the oaks and alders that stood over a stony brook beside the pub. A brown and trouty brook, noisy and still clear and clean, for the coal line lay beyond it, further down the valley. The road bridged the little brook and then bridged again the old canal, with its thick green mat of a face; a mat that moved when water rats moved, mysteriously green, bright, light, wet green, still, stagnant, and all about it the thick dark green of end-of-summer trees and the berries on the mountain ash and dog-rose slowly burning into autumn. He stood at the canal bridge and picked up a stone from the road and shied it at the greenness; the weeds hardly rippled, embracing the stone. He walked on towards the village where the mountain and the tips were conspiring together to keep out the last of the light. In the dusk it was hard to tell which was tip and which was rolling mountain, for the village tips were old, gone to grass, and losing the sharp lines that had, in the beginning, been as hard and assertive as a tart in falsies. The village pit was worked out and the miners went to earth under fresher fields and threw up newer, sharper tips, in other villages, in other valleys. Now there were no workings in Cilhendre, except for the small mines; small, private drifts, too insignificant for the Coal Board, but worth a man's while to work and make what he could of them. They were up on the mountain-sides and lost to sight in the embracing slopes, no more obtrusive from below than a gnat bite on a pretty girl's cheek.

The lights were on in the streets, but the houses seemed dark and untenanted; no lights shone in the front windows, for life was still centred on the back kitchen as it had always been. No small car or television could alter the fundamental class symbol of life in the back kitchen; the parlour was still reserved for death and courting. The houses were a jumble of different sorts. Terraced houses, built red-brick at the turn of the century, front doors opening on to the road and the life in them boiling out, public and inclusive, alike as matchboxes; a pretentious manse or two; a villa where the pound-pinching grocer's widow lived it out in dignity and Ciro pearls; then a sweep of semi-detached, pebble-dashed, bay-windowed, aspiring houses, called in a mad moment The Park Crescent and promptly renamed Rotten Row. The years had left their mark on Rotten Row.

Joe crossed another bridge, across the river that kept company with the village street. A friendly, pebbly river, where boys swam in summer, that folded itself in and out of the village, collecting tins and old saucepans as it went. Under the street lights the night had thickened and the river was a shiny black. On the middle of the old lattice-iron bridge a handful of small boys dressed in lumber jackets and blue jeans stuffed into Wellington boots saw Joe and ambushed him. 'Give us a penny for fireworks, Joe, only a month about to Guy Fawkes' and we haven't got nothing yet – not a penny, look. Please, Joe, only a penny to start us.'

'O.K., a penny it is, then, but save it, mind you. You can't get anything with a penny, so keep it till you get a few. Who's the treasurer?'

'Me,' five voices yelled and five dirty hands clawed towards him, while the other five fended off the nearest contender.

'You can't all be treasurer. One of you can be Chairman – you Geraint, you're the biggest; one has to be secretary – Sam, you're a scholar, aren't you? Then Wilf can be treasurer, 'cos he's the smallest and he'll be afraid to spend the penny. You two, Iorwerth and Islwyn, are the committee and the committee's job every morning is to ask the treasurer to show them the money. Here, Wilf, put it in this match-box and start to save. Sam, you scholar, you, if I give you a penny every day from now on till Guy Fawkes' how much will you have in pounds?'

'Pounds?' said Wilf, awed. 'Honest?'

'No, you clot, it'll be – it'll be thirty-one pennies, that's two and seven, Joe.' Sam was Steve Williams' youngest child, the one he called his second coming, his admirable after-thought. His eyes were large and round, under a jungle of fair curls, his nose had an impertinent tilt and his second teeth had come any old how.

'Right, Sam. Now, like I said, start saving. So long.'

'Thanks, Joe, mun, thanks.' They stood aside to let him pass, manly appreciation in their eyes for a bloke who was all right, and then they raced to huddle over the penny in the light from the window of the Italian's shop, where the stocks of fireworks were already mounting their temptations, and to calculate every best conceivable way of spending two and sevenpence.

Joe went on, pleased and happy with himself, and came to the chapel gate. There he stuck his big feet in their pointed shoes between the vertical iron bars of the gate and swung himself into the graveyard, and the gate jarred against the cracked, lichened headstone in memory of James Elias of this parish, Gone but not Forgotten, and Joe went in to the singing to 'Speak Comfortably to Jerusalem.'

CHAPTER 2

Sall Evans was a lonely woman. Though she lived at home with her mother and two brothers, and the neighbouring women dropped in for a chat, she was eaten up, tantalised, by her aloneness. She had been a lonely child, born late in life to an ailing mother, with her brothers already out of school and looking for work. Her father was killed when she was three, and sorrow and illness had isolated, wrapped, warped her mother. The boys were remotely older. At school the teachers said she was a strange child, sometimes bright and clever, sometimes lost in a deep, deep daze of misery, unable to concentrate, careless, uncaring. She made no friends at the school; sometimes she tried desperately to have a friend, but she tried too hard, talked too fast, chattered so compulsively that the children shied away. Her intensity, her hunger, was off-putting. The children sensed an oddness in her and she never had a best friend, never a special. She had nothing much to offer them; no beauty, no cleverness, no pretty dresses, no dirty stories, for her brothers were too old to pass them on, no secrets, no obvious advantages like being the minister's daughter, or the grocer's, nothing to offer but a moody devotion.

She had had only one young man, whom she met in a munitions factory towards the end of the war. He was, like her, away from home, medically unfit for the services; and in his misery Sall had been a comfort. They were married for a few years, but he was soon unfaithful to her, turning to another woman for 'some peace and quiet'. Then he left Sall and she came home to her mother's house – home, but an outsider, neither one of the proud wives nor one of the prouder girls.

She was thirty-six now and her life was given over to the care of her mother and to housekeeping for the two unmarried brothers. That, and reading *True Romances* and murders, and drinks at the pubs whose promise hypnotised her when *True Romances* palled. They were an undemonstrative family, the brothers ungiving, ignorant of gestures of tenderness, offers of gentleness, scornful of affection, cynical; and Sall lived with them, repressing her love, her warmth, clenching into fists the hands that only asked some other skin to touch, caress, have some sort of right to.

But she'd come to realise that there was something about her that communicated itself to men. There were men who knew by looking, catching on, that she was 'that sort', 'one of them'. She had to make no gesture, no indication; there was about her, around her, an acceptance, a servitude. She came to think of herself as belonging to a certain type of woman – she couldn't have been more explicit – a type whom men recognised; recognised as prey, as pleasure, as ease, as easy. She accepted the recognition, accepted its code. Men would talk to her and keep her company all evening in the pubs if she was kind to them afterwards, as long as she made no demands on them, asked only for talk and a minimum of politeness. They would treat her almost as an equal as long as she kept her head and never asked for more, never expected the empty words. By now she had learned to control her suicidal urge towards devotion.

While Joe Jenkins was at his singing practice, Sall came into the crowding bar of the Red Lion. A woman alone, in a grey summer coat and a cheap head-scarf patterned with a washed-out Buckingham Palace. She sat in the middle of the far wall, on a bench, and made a business lighting a cigarette and sorting in her handbag while she waited for Sam to come and ask for her order. She asked for gin and lime and looked around the bar for any familiar face, some token of recognition, as the Ancient Mariner might have searched and stared, then she took up her glass and twirled the silky, sticky contents round about and up and down the glass, with an assumption of indifference at her aloneness in that place of talkers. She took a paper-backed book from her bag, already open, with the pages that were read rolled over and under, dog-eared, second-hand. She bent her head to read, and as she reached the bottom of each page, looked around and then down again.

Joe came back to the pub after his rehearsal. He was in a queer mood, unpredictable to himself, tensed by the singing, ready to pick on someone or anyone, all organised for something, but only God knew what. His mood was elusive, like the end of a dream; the singing had taken him up somewhere and he didn't know how to come down. He thought a drink would help, but the pub was a different place. The confident quiet had been belched away with the froth of a hundred pints and the noise hit you coming in like a clout on the head. Class distinction had reared out its fat belly among the higher officials of the Coal Board, who wore wedding rings and drank whisky and hoped to buy a drink for the General Manager; but the General Manager had taken their measure and was enjoying a sly, unpretentious pint in Sam's quiet kitchen. High-pitched German voices were teaching the gin-and-tonic girls to say, 'Ich liebe dich' before 'Aufwiedersehen', and old colliers drank their pints and watched and spat on the floor. The air around the Germans was havana-grey, and thick woodbine-blue around the colliers. Steve had retreated to a corner and saw Joe at the door over the shoulders of the déclassé small-mine men with whom he was still souring his guts over Ben Butch's money. Joe saw the invitation in his one good eye. ''Scuse me, 'scuse me, please, let a bloke pass, then, move along there, please. Make a bit of room for a chap, then.' Sall watched him until she saw him join Steve and then her eyes went back to her page.

'Move up and give Joe an inch, will you, boys? Singing go all right, Joe?'

'Not bad. Any hopes of anything to drink, Steve?'

'You'll have to fight for it, boy, it's a bit late; you only got half an hour. What was you saying about the Russians now, Jim?' Steve turned his good eye towards Jim Kremlin, a little squit of a man with fair hair scattered over a bumpy head, smoke-brown ratty teeth and very brown, rolling eyes. Jim jabbed the thick air with a short, aggressive, assertive forefinger.

'Well, see, Steve, like I was saying, you can't get away from it, the Russians is right. It's all a problem of what you do with the profits. All right, you can make money in Russia. All right, but you invest it back in the State concerns, see. And then the profits, after you've had your dividend, fair enough, like the Co-op after all, the profits is invested back in the State, for the good of the community. That isn't capitalism, for God's sake.'

'But, Jim boy, what the hell is the good of the community? Hydrogen bombs?'

'If the Americans make bombs, Russia's got to defend herself, hasn't she? See the State Department letting the Communist State get on its feet if Russia didn't have bombs to threaten back with.'

'But Russia's aggressive, though, see? I'm the last man, God knows, to speak for the capitalist class, but Russia's at it all the time, mun. Won't leave anybody in peace.'

'Look, Steve,' Jim, doctrinaire, shifted his bottom another inch nearer Steve in his corner, 'that's only right; we can't let capitalism alone, world revolution won't happen if the underdogs get plenty in the capitalist society.'

'That kind of crap was all right before, Jim. It don't make sense any more. Honest it don't. This bloody bomb has changed everything, mun. It's put us back, right back in the middle ages. It's the mediaeval world all over again, when, one or two chaps was tin gods and all the rest didn't matter a damn. That's what we got now. Nobody cares a tinker's fart for you or me or Joe by here. We're nonentities, mun, votes or not. Let's change the subject. Sing for us, Joe, let's have a tune; come on, well have a song.'

'I haven't had a drink yet, what the hell.'

'Aye, change the subject. Can't you think about nothing but politics, Jim? And you can't talk either, working with us for old Ben Butch and his bit of private enterprise.'

'Good shot for you, Tom. You hit Jim by there.' Steve now rolled his good eye around to Tom Davies, Link. Link smirked in the glow of Steve's praise and buried his nose in his glass to hide his pleasure. Link was well named. His brow was low, his hair growing to within an inch of his eyebrows, and it was that sort of stiff, straight, black hair that would not take a parting, so that it hung down on his brow like a pelmet. His eyes were small, deep-set and pale seagrey and his nose spread all over the place like a leprous pygmy's. His upper lip was very long and jutting and his jaw heavily aggressive.

'Practising for your solo, is it, Joe?'

'Aye.'

'You in the choir, Tom?'

'Yes; not much go in the singing tonight, though, old Fred was cursing us from the pulpit; been a pretty place there if the preacher had walked in. Tamping mad old Fred was, the soperanos was swapping recipes half the time. No shape on anybody, somehow.'

Joe got up from the chair he was sharing with Link. 'I'm going to look for that drink. What you boys drinking?'

'Thanks, Joe, mun, Export all round it is.'

Joe broad-shouldered his way towards Sam behind the bar, but drew up like a dog on a short lead at the sight of Sall sitting alone on her bench, walled in by the backs of standing men. He bee-lined over to her. 'Hullo, Sall,' he said, 'long time no see. What you drinking?' He stood over her, his bulk between her and everything.

'Oh, hullo, Joe. You're looking well. Gin and lime, then, ta. How's tricks, Joe?' She looked up at him, smiling her troubled, twisted, kindly, insecure smile. Her eyes were huge, as though about to burst from the clench of the tight lids, huge and dark brown under a wide, clear brow, and her hair sprang back thickly, greying in two dramatic strokes on either side of her head, like a badger. But the rest of her face was unremarkable and her teeth were bad copies – in the Welsh have-them-all-out-and-save-trouble tradition. She held up her head to look at Joe and her neck showed thick and powerful, like a Norman pillar. There was a small, neat wen at the base of her throat. She closed her book as Joe went for the drinks and she lit another cigarette to hide from the encompassing backs the gladness in her face.

Joe fought his way back to Sam. 'Hullo, Joe, back then? Singing go all right?'

'Yes, thanks, Sam. Give us five Exports and a gin and lime, will you? Can you take four over to Steve's corner, with Mr Joe Jenkins' compliments? I'll take the other two.'

'O.K., Joe. I can try, whatever. Ta.'

'Still on the tea, Sam?'

'What d'you think boyo?'

'Well, give me the right change, whatever. I want that car, honest. Right, thanks, Sam.'

Sall squeezed herself small to make room for Joe when he came back, walking pigeon-toed to take less room and holding the drinks tight to his chest, like a forward breaking out of the scrum.

'Where've you been keeping, Sall? Been busy?'

'My mother was bad again and I've been a bit tied, but she's better now. You all right?'

'So so. Those Germans get on my nerves over there.'

'Why? They seem all right.'

'Not all right to the Jews, were they?'

'That's ancient history now, Joe, and anyway, most of those chaps are too young to know anything about it.'

'It's awful hot in here. Coming out for a breath of air?'

She put her hand over his. 'Don't be daft now, Joe, now you came in.'

'Well, I want to go out again. This pub has come to something. Look at it, Germans in one corner, bosses in the other, a revolution going on over there with Jim Kremlin, and every other bugger talking about the hydrogen bomb. Come on out, Sall, give us a break; I'm depressed.'

'There's no finesse about you at all, is there, Joe? A girl likes to keep up appearances. Talk to me for a bit. I haven't really heard human voices for weeks. My brothers hardly speak in the house – only to complain that there isn't enough salt or they want something different in their sandwiches. And my mother, God help her, can't get many words out at all since her stroke.'

'What would you like to talk about, then?'

'What have you been doing? Singing much?'

'I'm singing in Salem gymanfa in three weeks. That's where I've been tonight, to the practice. What you reading?'

'Only some old murder.'

Sam, with his stomach and his professional patter, bulldozed his way to Steve's corner. 'Here we are, gentlemen, four Exports. Joe's gone for a bit of a chat.' He winked at them and jerked his head at Sall, while he wiped the table-top and collected the empty glasses.

'Bit of all right, you mean, isn't it, Sam?'

'Oh, leave Joe alone, Tom; remember what he said about gathering rosebuds, Steve?' Sam left them, worldly wise and condescending.

'Not much of a bud, that one, is she? And I don't think much of Joe's choice of roses either.' Jim Kremlin dismissed roses, they hadn't a place in the dialectic.

'They say she's a good sort, mind you, Jim.' Steve had a vast tolerance for anyone who wasn't rich.

'Good for what, Steve?' Link said, his little eyes bright with dirt and envy.

'Well, judge not that ye be not judged, Tom bach. Takes all sorts, doesn't it? Well, here's to Joe.' He looked over towards them but Joe was engrossed and didn't notice when they drank his health.

She was saying, 'Did you sing well?'

'All right, see. Have another one, Sall, drink up, it's nearly stop-tap. Same again, is it?'

'All right, then. Thanks.'

'Don't move, will you? Don't go away.'

'O.K., Joe, I won't run away.' She smiled the same half-promising, half-frightened smile and he went to collect the drinks, his thoughts in abeyance, his mood now translated, given over, to his body's needs, his soul centred below his belt, his eyes slightly glazed, his breath already heavy and deep and his voice thicker and furred.

'Drink up, Sall, drink up, and let's get out of here. There's a good girl.'

'Look, Joe, I'm not going out with you. You go first. Go natural and I'll follow when I've finished my fag. Take it easy now, Joe boy.'

'Promise you'll follow, won't you? Be a pal.'

'Yes, I'll follow you, honest. By the time you're out of the Gents I'll be outside.'

'I'll wait outside the door, then. Don't take all night over that fag, will you?' He gave her his chopped-off half-wave, nodded to Steve's corner and swung out of the door, young and urgent. As he waited for her in the fresh, crisp dark in the shadow of the porch over the door of the pub, his mind still thumping with the tremendous music, his soul aware of itself, of its loneliness, of the deep sky and the stars and the shapes of trees, he gave no thought to Sall as Sall. He felt himself awake to the night, pricked like an adolescent by the eternal magic, the magnificence. He might, in other circumstances, in other worlds, have written it, sung it, but this that he would do was easier, simpler, direct. The woman was part of the night, the luck of the night, the pool for the leaping salmon.

She ground out the butt of her cigarette, smoothed out her dress and, tying up her headscarf again, went, modest and unassuming, out to Joe. 'There you are, Sall. Oh, Sall, come here, give us a kiss. That's something to be going on with. Take that old scarf off, it spoils you.' He put his arm across her shoulders and they swung across the plank bridge, across the trouty stream.

'What if your girl saw you now, Joe?'

'Who, Cyn? I'm not sure she is my girl, if you want to know.'

'Quarrelled, then?'

'No, but there's a German she's interested in, been out with him a few times. Jenkins doesn't like it.'

'Was he there tonight?'

'I don't know; that's what I was wondering. I don't know him myself – but don't talk about her. You're nice, Sall. How that husband of yours could leave you beats me, honest.'

'Good riddance. He wasn't much cop, Joe. I'm better without him, more myself. Only I feel lonely sometimes, like I told you before, and once a girl's been married, well, it's different than a single girl, see.'

'Shall we go down the canal bank, Sall?'

'I mustn't be long. I'll have to catch the eleven o'clock bus.'

'I wish I had enough to buy that car. I could drive you home then.'

'Still saving?'

'Trying to. Shall we sit down? Here, sit on my coat. All right? Not cold are you?' Sall was kind, accessible, sympathetic and simple. She was too experienced and not pretty

enough to put up formalities and conventional hurdles. She
liked Joe, he was a friend, and sex was only a gesture of
friendship, only one way to be nice, a way to say thank you
for company and conversation. She was helpful and relaxed,
but she never let go – not now – she watched and appreciated, but tried to stand aside. She knew she had to give passivity; she concentrated on passivity as other women, the loved
women, concentrated on fulfilment; this was one of the disciplines of loneliness.

Joe, she prayed to herself, Joe, say something, say anything. Say Darling, only once, even Sall; Sall, for me to know
it's me, say something, the sea is coming in, oh the sea, the
sea, watch yourself, Sall, the sea's coming in, it's coming in,
coming in, oh, the tide, the seaside. Oh, Joe.

Joe was alone, the singing in his guts was coming out,
easy, I don't like the feel of her teeth, like Sam's missus, keep
my tongue to myself. Take it easy, Joe, Oh, God, don't rush
it, God. Please give me time, time, time, oh, God, it's from
my toe-nails. Christ!

He opened his eyes and saw in that magnificent, momen-
tary clarity the black-green grass, smelt autumn, smelt rain.
Like one who listens to the sorrow in the reeds – how does it
go on? – the sorrow in the reeds, amidst the laughter of his
lover in the moonlight, I think the thoughts of dull old age –

'Come on, Joe, boy. I've got to catch my bus.'

– before the coming of my sad decay.

'Joe, will you move, it's late, honest.'

What's she talking about, wish she'd shut up. 'All right,
Sall, all right. Give us a minute.'

She stretched back and reached for her bag and lit two cigarettes. 'Come on, have a fag, look. Have a drag before we
go.'

'Thanks, Sall.' He moved, lay back and smoothed away
his hair from his face; he put his hand on her knee and
pressed it. 'You're a nice girl, Sall, you know that?'

'Come here, let me clean your mouth, it's probably covered with lipstick. Here, spit on my hankie and I'll wipe it off. There you are, boy, clean and tidy once again.'

'Thanks, Sall; better go, I suppose,' but he still made no effort to move. The tension of the singing drowned in a deep pool, his soul back where it belonged, he lay slack and eased on his back in the grass, while Sall picked bits of twigs and dried autumn out of her underwear and combed her hair. She kissed him again, quickly, gently. 'Come on now, Joe, I've got to catch that old bus.'

CHAPTER 3

Jim Kremlin worked his heading in the small mine at Brynhyfryd with his fellow traveller Dai Dialectic. They were telling each other what a great man Stalin had been, after all, as they propped up their roof and wedged the props firmly, skilfully in the low darkness. Their heading was only four feet in the best places and the seeping surface-water dripped continuously about them as they knelt there in the hot, dusty dark. They were both good colliers, taking pride in their roofing and in the proper organisation of their stall, as a housewife is proud of a well-organised, uncluttered kitchen.

Dressed only in their trousers and singlets, their bodies looked small and insignificant in the darting, narrow lights of the lamps they wore on their steel helmets; the lights played, flickered momentarily over the shining blackness of the coal wall before them, on the dull iron of the tram they were filling, on the grey Pennant granite of the roof and the warm, brown, flaking bark of the pit-props. Then the lights moved and all was blind again. Their tram stood on two rails that were almost submerged under the black water that dripped, dripped all about and around.

'Oh, no, we haven't heard the last of old Stalin yet, come you, he'll get fair play yet. You can't quarrel with history, see, Dai.'

'That's right enough, too.'

'There's two trams filled already, boyo; not doing bad today. Have a tidy handful of quid to collect Friday.'

'Aye. Hey, what's that? Can you hear something? Hush a minute; I can hear quarrelling. Listen.'

'Aye, you're right. Down tools, boyo, I want to hear this.'

'Link it is – Link and Ben Butch, I think.'

'Shall we go and have an earful?'

'Aye, come on; it's time we had a snap, anyway.'

They slung their jackets over their shoulders and crept on hands and knees out of their heading, dodged the full trams and sloshed through the dark water, single file between the tram lines, calling out occasionally in case someone should send an empty journey down as they came along. The roof was still low and they walked with their heads bent forward, anthropoid, black, their arms swinging low, their lights directed at their feet, at the black, busy water.

They drew nearer the raised, angry voices and at a junction of the roads, when daylight was a promised pin-prick ahead of them, they saw two bobbing head lamps that jerked swathes, waves, scatterings of perspectives around the darkness, a stripe across the grey flank of an old, rock-still colliery horse, a shine on the rock roof, a catching of the diamond drips, the wild-eyed, black faces, the motes, the beams of dust.

Ben Butch, the owner of the mine, and Tom Davies, Link, were damning and blasting each other across the back of the little grey horse and Krem and Dai Dialectic stopped in their tracks beyond the parting to enjoy the fight.

'Want me to loose my bloody licence or what? We'll have the N.C.B. down our throats like a ton of bricks for this. I've told you enough where the boundary is, damn you to hell.'

'You bloody shout enough if we don't get the damn coal, if we don't fill your effing trams. There's good coal there, easy to get, and who the hell's to notice we've gone beyond our allocation?'

'The NC bloody B. That's who. We was warned before and this new General Manager will jump on us, give him half a chance. I've been told, mun, he's only looking for the chance, what the hell. And I've told you too, often enough.'

The little horse flicked her tail and Link stroked her, turning on a new voice as he absent-mindedly addressed her.

'There you are, bach, it's all right, lovie,' as though she were an indulged female child. 'Look here, boyo, if you're not satisfied with my work down by here, you know what you can do with your bloody job. You can stuff it, see, and go and screw yourself.'

'Damn, don't you talk to me like that, Tom Davies; you'll soon see who's boss around here. All right, then, I'll take your offer; you can come for your cards now and you can bugger off whenever you like. Come on you, your cards are in the office. Take them and stuff them.'

'See you getting coal without a bloody fireman, good boy, you'll have to close down, boyo. I can get another job tomorrow, but it'll be down tools here without me, stop shop for you. And you needn't come begging me to come back, not on your Nelly; I've had you, Ben Butch, and I wants my week's wage in lieu.' Link moved out towards the daylight, giving the little horse a lingering farewell caress as he went, and Ben shouted after his bowed and lumbering back, 'Glad to give it, too. There's no swine indispensable in this place. Go on, get out of my bloody sight.' He turned away from Link and his light caught the faces of Jim and Dai behind the empty trams. 'What do you two think you're doing by there behind the trams? You're supposed to be cutting that coal, you are.'

'Coming out for a snap, Ben, that's all. Krem and me wants a fag, see. We filled two down there. You coming out?'

'Aye, I'm coming to give that dirty monkey his cards. Know of a fireman looking for a job?'

'Firemen is hard to find these days.'

'I'll find one. I'd rather close this bloody pit than see that Link another day.'

They climbed the steady incline to the top, one behind the other. The drift was steep at this point, following the line of the coal seam, and they had to save all their wind for walking. They walked in a heavy silence, lumbering out. In the light at last, they stood still for a moment in the sun and the blessedly fresh air, the lights in their helmets a mockery in the clear, crisp brightness of the October morning.

The mine was high above the village, a pockmark on the gentle slope of the fawn mountainside. There was no complicated machinery on the top. Natural ventilation and no depth made fans and cages unnecessary; this coal, sold direct to industry, required no screening and the only equipment they needed was the trams, the lines and a small chute down which the coal could be bounced and bounded into a lorry parked below. There was a small diesel engine to produce compressed air for the drillings; it stood battered and yellow and a little rusty beside a shelter leaning into the mountainside. In this shelter a brazier glowed and made the air heave and the lorry-driver was boiling a kettle on it. Jim Kremlin and Dai Dialectic walked towards him, lighting their cigarettes and feeling for their food boxes, sloshing and skidding in their Wellington boots through the water that seeped everywhere. Ben Butch stood at the mouth of the drift. He was a big man, run to fat, with a big, slack belly aggressively pregnant over his leather belt and a thick, suspicious bull neck. He stood at the mouth of the drift, looking for something, somebody else to spew the last dregs of his anger at, his short upper lip pulled down under the snub nose and his lower lip pushed out, wet, red, in his coal grimed face. Link was standing at the door of the little shed which was the colliery office. 'What about them cards?' he shouted. 'Changed your mind?'

'Catch me.' Ben Butch moved over to the office, heavy, ugly, menacing, like an armoured car in a silent street. He pushed past Link into the minute office which was little more than a cover for the weighing machine, the telephone and the framed card of safety regulations over which Ben hung his coat. He found the employment cards, sorting them in his thick, insensate, black sausage fingers and then held Link's out to him. 'Here you are, take it – and look sharp, myn uffern i, before I give you something to go with it.'

'Think you're great, don't you? You won't be so bloody cheerful tomorrow, when there's nobody here to do your dirty work for you. So long, you old screwer. And don't forget my wages. Send them down tomorrow.' Link threw down his steel helmet and his battery. The battery fell, heavy, into the black coal-mud around the office door, while the helmet bounced on its length of cable on to a tram line and then floated upside down like a little boat on the black pool between the lines. Link went bounding down the slope, his arms loose, his legs bowed, underlining in the sunlight the horrid aptness of his nickname.

Ben Butch crossed the mud to the shelter where the men, in silence until the end of the storm, were making tea. 'We'll have to find another fireman, boys; anybody got any ideas?' Ben was now more placatory, he couldn't afford to lose any more men.

'I been thinking, Ben: you know young Joe Jenkins, Bryn Flossie's son? He's a good little boy. Got his Second Class Certificate. He was saying the other night he wouldn't mind making a bit more money, down the Red Lion he was. Go and have a word with him. No harm in trying, whatever.'

'Bryn Flossie's boy? That chap that plays hooker for Cilhendre?'

'Well aye, mun, you know Joe, for God's sake. Sings a bit.'

'Aye, I know who you mean now. Think he'd come?'

'You can try him, and you can't afford to wait, can you? There's only a few day's work left here now, if you don't get a fireman. And he'll have to serve his notice with the N.C.B. like.'

'When will he be home, Krem?'

'Mornings he's working.'

'I'll try him, whatever. Decent fellow, is he?'

'Aye, good sort, old Joe. Bit of a boy, mind. Saw him going off with old Sall Ever Open Door the other night as bold as brass.'

'He can pick his greens wherever he likes, only do some work here after. I'll go and see him tonight, then. Got a cup of tea there, Cyril?'

Cyril was the lorry driver, starkly clean and tidy among the colliers – so clean that he looked sickly beside them. He was a neat, fussy little man with a face like a fat baby-doll and he wore a yellow toupee, the only toupee in the whole valley, as far as anyone knew. He had no inhibitions about his toupee; he was very proud of it and was always prepared to lend it out for concerts and carnivals and dramas. He wasn't fussy where he wore it; sometimes he had a high intellectual brow, sometimes his brow was more like Link's.

He passed Ben a thick earthenware mug filled with rust-coloured tea stiff with sugar. The men crouched on their haunches over the tea, looking primitive, like witches or savages. The colliers rinsed their mouths out with the first tastes and spat carefully, accurately, through pursed lips at an empty tin which was floating, lopsided, in the same puddle as Link's hat. The spit hit the jack every time, like darts, and the tin rocked in the water, catching the sun.

'Kids all right, Ben?' Cyril asked. He was a bachelor and a great man for families.

'Aye, thanks. That Link's a swine, though, isn't he, mun?'

'I never liked Link somehow, got a face like a blackleg.'

'Tidy wife though, mind you. Fat, granted, but she's a good old sort. Too good for Link, him and his bloody pigeons.'

'Fancy going to bed with Link, though, fair play.'

'I rather not think about it, thank you.' Cyril was horrified.

'Cyril's not interested in bed, are you, Cyril?'

'Leave him alone, Krem; what about those two trams you say you filled? Two more would fill the lorry, wouldn't they, Cyril?'

'Aye, bring them up and I can go. I don't like the remarks some people make. Russia indeed, and no family life or nothing.'

'Come on then, boys. We left Bluebell in the cut. She can bring those two up nice.'

'Righto then, let's go. Better save that helmet of Link's, Ben. You might get another fireman and he'll want a helmet, whoever he is.'

'Where's your matches, Krem? I didn't see you putting them down.'

'Think I'm daft or what? There they are, on that ledge.'

'Right. Everybody else left their matches? Come on then.'

They bowed their heads and went back to the mouth of the drift, back to the wet, intimate darkness, and left Cyril in the shed, the October sun shining on his toupee and on the yellow leaves of a little, slender willow tree that grew out of the mountain rocks by the side of the shelter, coy as a bunch of cherries on an Edwardian hat.

CHAPTER 4

Wilf took the match-box out of his pocket and rattled it softly to hear the pennies. Old Fatty Wilks was going on and on about some old desert. He hadn't been listening for some time now and the sun was making his eyes heavy and tired. Fatty's voice was going on and on, like a busy bee trapped on a window. She was a nasty old teacher, one of the fat, old, ugly ones. Her hair was all done, up in plaits, like a gypsy woman, and her old eyes could see through your mind like a dose of senna. She must think that old blue overall was hiding her figure a treat, but it was too tight on her old bum and her old tits. Fatty. Old English Fatty. The money moved gently in the box.

'Wilfred, what have I been saying during the last five minutes? Bring me whatever it is you're playing with. Come along, bring it out, look sharp.'

'I wasn't playing with nothing, Miss.'

'Come on, bring it out.' She stood with her fat, pink, soft hand out. 'Bring it here, I say.'

'I can't, Miss. It is'n' mine. I'm only keeping it for my butties.' Wilf tried to stuff the box back, but it stuck in the broken lining of his pocket.

'Are you defying me, Wilfred Thomas?' She duck-wobbled up the gangway to Wilf's place. 'Let me see it. Matches? Matches?' She clipped him across the ear and his head rolled round with the swing of it.

Sam Williams, Secretary of the Guy Fawkes' Savings Committee, stood up in his place and put up his hand.

'Please, Miss.'

'Yes, Samuel.' Old Sam was a bit of a pet because he got his sums right.

'It's not matches, Miss, it's only a match-box, Miss. It's a money-box, like. To save up in.'

She opened the precious Swan match-box and took out two sixpences and two pennies. 'Oh, very creditable, I'm sure, but I cannot have Wilfred Thomas playing with match-boxes or money-boxes in my lesson. Here you are, Samuel, take the box and the pennies and put them right away, out of sight, and I will keep the two sixpences and give you a savings stamp in return. That will be far safer than your box. Collect another ten pennies and you can have another pretty stamp. I'll give you a savings card to keep, with your names on it. We'll excuse you this once, Wilfred; you may both sit down and get on with the exercise on the Gobi Desert. Well, Samuel, I told you to get on.'

'But, Miss, we don't want to save – I mean, we don't want stamps. We want to spend it.'

'You think of nothing but spending in the modern generation. You must be taught the advantages of thrift. Why, in five years' time this shilling will be worth one and a penny ha'penny.'

Geraint, as Chairman of the Savings Committee, shouted from the back seat into the stunned silence, 'My father said we'll all be blown to hell in five years, so it's no good saving. Eat, drink and be merry, he said, for tomorrow we'll surely die. An' in five years' time I'll be earning good money, I expect, and I'll be able to give you a penny ha'penny if you're going to be hard up when you retire. My father said you ought to be retiring any day now, he said.'

The girls in the class were accomplished diversionists. 'Oh, Miss, what will you do when you retire? Will you have a little house by yourself, and a garden and that? Though they say that Old People's Home is very nice in Pontardawe. Used to be the Workhouse, but they painted it.'

'My grannie wants to go there. Anywhere's better than with us, she said. Too many children with my mother. Ten, and I'm only number four.'

'Will you have a cat when you retire, Miss? Company when you haven't got a husband.'

'Our cat's had kittens, we kept two and drowned two. You can have one of them when it's opened its eyes, if you like, Miss. The ginger one is best. Ginger cats is the best fighters, but tortoise is always girls.'

'Tortoises isn't always girls, or you couldn't have baby tortoises, then, could you, Miss?'

Biology was taboo in Miss Wilks' class. 'Silence!' she bellowed. 'Get on with your exercise. No more talking. I'll make out your savings card while you answer those questions on page 39.'

Wilf was crying, his red head down on his arm over the geography book on his desk. He didn't have a hankie because a hankie was cissie. Crying was cissie, too, but he couldn't help it. It was the end of the world. Two whole sixpences, and that old cow, bitch, damn bugger, had pinched them. He kicked the front of his desk and suddenly jumped out of his place and charged to the front of the class, his face red and streaming and working like yeast.

'Give me our money back, you old thief. It's not your money. Give it back.' He pulled at her old blue overall, rocking her. 'Give it back, or I'll tell the polices, and my father. My father's bigger than you, and I'll tell Joe – Joe can fight you, and your old cane.'

She took hold of him by his ear as though he was something too disgusting to touch, as though he was at the end of a pair of tongs, and dragged him outside to the corridor while the whole class sat in excited, terrified, titillated horror. 'Come to the headmaster, my child, he will deal with this.' Her voice went deep and hollow, like a stone down a well. Wilf kicked her, but she was bigger and fatter than he was, her grip on his ear was like a pair of pliers. The headmaster, who was teaching the scholarship class, heard hell breaking loose in the corridor and burst from his class like fizz from a bottle. He was a kindly, ageing Socialist whose gods were Marx and Lenin, with Tolstoy to make up the Trinity and D. H. Lawrence as a seraph in close attendance. He was as bald as a monk, with the face of a saint and patience to everlasting with kids. His hatred of violence was almost pathological and old Miss Wilks was one of his heaviest crosses.

'Well, well, what is it now? What is it? What's gone wrong?'

Wilf's fighting bantam blood was up. 'I had a shilling and Miss took it for a stamp and I don't want her old stamp and it isn't my shilling. So I called her a thief 'cos she won't give it back and she can't make me save if I don't want. And she hit me over the head and it's against the law, so I kicked her back and it was self-defence.'

Miss was still struggling to get her breath back and her hair into the net, when Wilf saw the master smother a grin with suddenly tightened lips.

'Leave this to me, Miss Wilks,' he said, and took young Robespierre Thomas to his room. 'Now look here, Wilf,' he said when they were both seated, 'you know you can't carry on like this in school. You must do what the teacher tells you, you know that.'

'Yes, sir. But look here, sir, she didn't have no business taking my money – our money, I mean – it's our savings and we don't want her old stamps. You can't spend old stamps.'

'Where did you get the money then, Wilf?'

'Off Joe, Joe Jenkins Flossie. He's been giving us a penny every day to save for fireworks only he gave us thrippence yesterday 'cos he's starting a new job and he's left Cefn Coed and he gave us the thrippence 'cos he was celebrating. And I don't see why old Miss has got any right to pinch it.'

'Well, it's for your own good, to teach you to save.'

'But we was saving, though, that's why I had it in my match-box, and she stole it.'

'She didn't steal it, Wilf, she's only keeping it for you.'

'Look, sir,' Wilf looked around the untidy room for a practical example. 'Look, if I took this book from by here and kept it for you and you was wanting to read it, you wouldn't like it, I bet. You'd say I was a thief all right.'

'Well, now, Wilf, you must have been playing about with the money or Miss Wilks wouldn't have seen it, so you couldn't have been attending properly. So you'll write out a hundred times, "I must attend in class." And you'll stay behind after school till you finish. Now here's a shilling and I want you to keep it for me till you get the money back from the stamp. Keep the stamp safe, and when you take it to the Post Office and get your money, you can give me back my shilling, see?'

'Yes, sir. Can I spend your shilling, or have I got to keep it? If I keep it for five years, I'll lose it for certain sure.'

'No, you can spend it, but you'll owe it to me. All right?'

'Yes, sir. Ta, sir.'

'Now, sit down by my desk and start on those lines and you don't go home till you've done them. Did Joe tell you what his new job was?'

'He's gone to Ben Butch's small mine, to make money. He's saving up for a car, he said. P'raps he'll give us a ride. I'll tell him you lent us a shilling and then p'raps he'll give you a ride too, sir.'

'Well, we'll see. Get on now then. There's pencil and paper. Tidy writing, mind.'

'Yes, sir. Sir, I can't spell "attend".'

'Put "listen", then. No, not lissen, there's a "t" in the middle, l-i-s-t-e-n. Get on now and don't you move from there till I come back. I'll be in Standard 7, if anybody wants me.'

Wilf's finger was cramped with pressing on the pencil long before the bell rang for the end of school. His back was sore with bending over the master's high table and his head was spinning with 'I musts' and there were still hundreds more old lines to do. He heard the thunder of the released children, leaving him to that complete silence that overtakes a school when it is abandoned to the cleaning women and the caretaker. Then, there was a furtive tap at the master's window and Wilf looked up to see four scared faces apparently balancing on the window sill. He put down his pencil, and, without moving from his place or saying one word, he took the precious shilling from his pocket and held it up to his friends, between his thumb and forefinger. Then he put it back in his pocket, clapped his hand over it and gave the thumbs-up sign and went back to his writing, like a busy man. The faces melted from the window, and outside it the four committee members punched each other for joy and tramped off home to tea, arm in arm, singing at the tops of raucous, coarse, hoarse, small-boy voices:

'Ask your mother for sixpence
To see the new giraffe.
A pimple on his whiskers,
A pimple on his Ask your mother for sixpence.'

CHAPTER 5

Joe walked home down Railway Street through the fine, diligent, determined rain. Railway Street was a row of small semi-detached, bay-windowed, identical houses. In all the houses the curtains were of the same kind, if not quite the same shade, of fawn-rust, neat, uninspired, with a frill along the top; the furniture in the parlours was all of a pattern: a china cabinet with Shelley ware in it, a coffee set, strictly for display, on an adjacent trolley, a fat 'three-piece' and a vase of artificial flowers on the windowsill. The natural human urge for a little particular variety was satisfied by the fantastic Welsh names given to the houses. 'The Court where the Nightingale Sings' sat cheek by jowl with 'The Pleasant Headland'; 'Snowdon' shared a party wall with 'Dovey's Banks'; and the 'Linnet's Bush' suffered from the faulty lavatory overflow of 'The White Winter Home'.

'Snowdon' was Link's house and as Joe passed the window Link himself stood there, hidden by the pale rust curtains. He stood in his shirt-sleeves and stockinged feet and watched Joe from the shadows; he clenched his hands and glowered, malignant as a gorilla. 'That bastard,' he said.

Joe went on down the road, his whole body swinging to the rhythm of the clumsy clumping of his heavy, hob-nailed boots. His working trousers tied at the knees and rigid with a dried paste of mud and coal-dust, the food tin and water bottle that he carried in his jacket pockets pushed the coat out, held it away from his body, like small flying buttresses, and his black face under the pulled-over cap was melodramatic in its contrasts, the large eyes bright, vivid, alive

41

and the teeth a white flash in the black, blanketing mask, mat, of dust.

His shouted 'hullo' at the back door brought his mother running out to watch him take off the inhuman, hard, oiled, weighted boots at the door. 'So it hasn't killed you, then, your first day, boy?'

'Not quite, Mam, but I'm not far off dead. Never mind, roll on pay day.' He trotted lightly into the kitchen in his stockinged feet and washed some of the dirt off his face and hands over the kitchen sink. He wasn't properly clean and tracks of coal still lay along his eyelids and in the creases around his nose and mouth. 'Got a good feed ready? I'm starving.' He sat on a kitchen chair with a page of the *Daily Herald* for a cushion and a sheet of the *Western Mail* for a table-cloth.

'It's like old times, Joe, to see a collier looking like a collier, honest. Am I a bit daft, or what? – but I feel you're more of a man in your dirt, like.'

'If you don't serve that food quick, I won't be half a man. I'm bloody ravenous. Dad home?'

'Yes, he's doing his sniffs in the parlour; I couldn't have him here under my feet when I had your dinner to get. It might taste of menthol.'

'How's he taking it today that I've gone to Ben's? Reconciled, is he?'

'Can't say he is really, Joe. I don't know what he's belly-aching about, I'm sure, something about you deserting the Coal Board and doing the dirty on nationalisation.'

'Oh, balls to that. He's been talking to Steve Williams, that one's saying the same, but I want the extra cash. Dad's too old-fashioned, and Steve's been getting at him; but I'll go back when we've got this coal out. For God's sake, what's he shouting about?'

Oh, well, don't start arguing tonight, whatever, let's have a minute's peace in the place. Got a rehearsal tonight?'

'No, ducks, I got a date with Cynthia. I said to myself, pride's all right, Joe, but it's no fun, so I phoned her up from Ben's place. Is my best shirt clean?'

'Your Italian shoes are with Idris the Boots, mind.'

'Lord, I forgot. I wonder if he's done them. Mam, you couldn't go and ask him, could you while I have a bath? Be a sport, will you?'

'Well, I'll ask, but he hates to be rushed, that one, he'll probably throw me out, and if he's drunk he might throw the shoes after me.'

'Try, will you, then? This bit of food is nice, Mam, got a pudding?'

'Here you are, gutsy, apple tart. I'll go to Idris's then.' She threw a shabby blue coat over her shoulders, picked up her tomato-red plastic handbag and went off, still in her curlers, through the fine rain to the cobbler's. At the back door, she turned to Joe, 'Cut us a bucket of coal before you change, will you? Oh, aye, and don't let me forget to tell you about Mrs Link. She's declared war.'

Joe lit a cigarette and read the Births, Marriages and Deaths column in his table-cloth as he savoured the smoke and drew it deep into his lungs. Bryn came out of the parlour, practising breaths.

'Hullo, boy, thought I heard you. All right over there, was it?'

'Aye, fine; plenty to cut there, more than they're finding in Cynheidre, whatever. And no bosses and no schemes and no systems. O.K. by me, Pop, it'll do me fine while it lasts.'

'Yes, boy; and no proper safety precautions, no organisation and no sense of working in a community and for your community.'

'Dad, I've heard those words before; Steve's been giving you lessons, but it's too late to start on that tack now. Give it a rest, look, till this coal's worked out and then I'll go back,

honest I will. I promised Mam I'd cut some coal before I
wash. Better do it or she'll start.' He pushed away his plate,
threw away his cigarette butt and went out to the coal shed in
the garden: Bryn pottered indecisively around, fingering the
ornaments and vaguely looking over the dusty bits of paper,
bills and old letters that Flossie had stuck behind the battered
Staffordshire figurine in the middle of the mantelpiece, a figurine of a thin, red retriever who had lost one of his legs and
all his dinner. Bryn had long since given up crossing swords
with either Flossie or Joe when any crisis arose, contenting
himself with muttered grumbles and oblique references to his
own inferior position in the family: that nobody listened to
him and that he was no more than a working ornament in that
house.

While Joe hammered away at the coal, Link, two gardens
down the road, was talking to his pigeons in their loft. Once
again he was able to watch Joe and keep himself hidden.
Enclosed and secure in the pigeon warmth, he could let his
face go as he looked at the boy whom he now considered his
enemy, the one who had robbed him of his bread and butter,
for he had been confident that Ben Butch would come cap-
in-hand to ask him to return to Brynhyfryd. Link threw a
pigeon out of his hand to make a fist and shook it at the
unconscious, hammering, young Joe. He was a good hater,
was Link, and obscurely glad of an obvious and positive
object for the besetting emotion in whose territories he
moved most confidently. He looked up towards his own
house and saw his wife at an upstairs window. She, too, was
watching Joe, and as Link watched she put out a huge, fat
arm to pull the window to and fastened it with a bang, as
though to shut out the sight of Joe, of his strong, muscular,
dirty arms, and to deaden the sound of his hammering.
'There's another one,' Link said to his pigeons, and gently
stroked one of them on its warm, purple-grey breast, feeling
the heat there under the feathers, the smooth, smooth outside

feathers and the sudden, surprising, harsh stalks close to the giving skin. He could feel the heart-beat.

His hatred of his wife had become an everyday emotion with him; he hated her vast body and her dough-coloured, squashed, ageing face, but he had to have a woman and nobody else would have him. Nobody else would have her, either; it was a terrible alliance of the undesired, fostered in lust and cemented with hate and contempt on his side, but with patient, unswerving loyalty on hers; she had never dared to dream of marriage and he had come; she owed to him marriage, a home, a man of her own. She was grateful.

But he hated her. He hated her when he made love to her, buried himself in her fat, and enjoyed it better because she knew he hated her, despised her.

Joe filled the coal buckets and chopped up a pile of pit-prop ends for firewood. When he padded back to the kitchen again, Bryn had fallen asleep in his armchair, his head thrown back, his mouth open and his big scarred hands touching the floor on either side of his chair. Joe was moved to pity and sympathy, but was too scared of sentimentality to acknowledge such feelings, and as he watched his father, even while he pitied, he went through a silent pantomime of throwing a penny into the open, pathetic, noisy mouth. But he took care not to disturb his father and went silently out of the room and upstairs to his bath. Getting the coal off in a bath he found surprisingly more difficult than getting clean under the showers at the pit-head, for, though he could soak in a nice big bath of hot water, the coal dust floated to the top of the water and little particles clung to his skin and there was no way of swishing them away. In the end he had to trust to the towel to remove them. He rubbed himself with the rough towels till his skin almost itched, dreaming idly of Cynthia, of women, of warmth as he stood there. He pulled the plug out of the bath, but made no attempt to clean it of the coal; cleaning baths was a woman's work and there are no greater respecters of the division of labour than the colliers. Cut coal and sticks, yes, but wash a dish or make a meal if there was a woman to do it, not on your little Nelly.

Flossie had put his cleaned and mended shoes in his bedroom and his best shirt was laid on the bed. The shirt had a lovely feel on his clean skin – smooth, like a girl's thighs. As he stood in his shirt, fixing his tie in the mirror, he saw his hands and, thinking of thighs, he turned his hands over and looked at them hard; then he ran his hands along his own naked thighs and shook his head, they were gone beyond repair. The coal in them was in for ever, every underground cut and gash he'd ever had was etched there for good, for coal stays put in colliers' cuts. God, they were rough; poor Cyn.

His father was awake when Joe came downstairs, talking idly to Flossie. 'Looking smart, boy, going somewhere special?'

'Got a date with Cyn, Dad. What's the time?'

'Oh, it's early yet, Joe bach. When you meeting her?'

'Seven, by the square in Cwmtwrch. I'll have to catch the bus; twenty-past six, isn't it, Mam?'

'Yes, sit down a minute.' He sat on the edge of a hard kitchen chair, his knees apart, his hands dangling, relaxed, between them, his elbows on his knees. He turned to Flossie, 'You got my shoes, then; thanks.'

'That's eighteen shillings you owe me, boyo. I had a job getting them too. Old Idris has gone on the cruse. He was lying there on top of all those smelly old boots, sleeping it off, when I went up. But he hadn't locked his door so I went in to see if I could find them myself. Ych y fi, the smell in there would drop you, honest; drinking meths he'd been, his breath was nearly coming out purple. Strike a match and he'd go – whoosh, so long Idris, see you in the next world. Between the smell of meths and leather and other people's old boots, it was coming to meet you in the door, mun. He was out for the count was Idris, so I didn't risk waking him, but I poked around a bit, tiptoe, and I found your shoes, all ready and the price on the label, so I picked them up and left the money. Eighteen bob. There's money to charge for tapping, you could have nearly bought two new pairs before the war for that. And he's got a nerve too, that Idris. Know what he had on the label? Joe Bryn Menthol if you please. I'll give him menthol when he wakes up, him and his old meths. That's you again,' she turned on Bryn, 'given the boy a nickname now.'

'Well, it's a bit of a change, anyway; most people call me Joe Jenkins Flossie, so you can't say much yourself, Mrs Jenkins. Oh, yes, you told me to remind you to tell us about Mrs Link declaring war.'

'Well, indeed to God, I nearly forgot. Yes, this morning it was, see, the fruit cart came, about ten it'd be, and I goes out for a bit of fish. Plate in my hand, doing no harm. Well, I bought this bit of hake for supper, see, and then I fancied a few bananas and odds and ends and then I saw those musher-rooms you had with your dinners. So I said, Oh well, once in a lifetime, Flossie, and took a quarter. When I was struggling down those old steps Sammy Fish's got into his old bus, mun, I dropped the blooming musher-rooms and of course they rolled all over the pavement and there was me and a couple of dogs in the rain trying to decide what to do about them when who should come wobbling and flopping down the road, mun, but Mrs Link. She saw me and my musher-rooms. Course, one look at her and the dogs had vanished. She comes up, see, and sniffs and all her double chins jerked like jelly and she said, 'Some people can afford to throw musher-rooms away, thanks to taking other people's jobs and livelihoods; blacklegs can have musher-rooms and hake, and others are lucky to have a herring between two.' I can see her and Link sharing a herring, not half!

"'I'm not throwing them away, Nell," I said, quick as you please, "you needn't hope. I'm going to pick up everyone of them, but here's two each for you and Tom, go nice with the herring. Stretch it for you." And she wobbled off, mun, up the steps, and the old bus nearly had a flat tyre with the weight of her. When she got to the top of the steps, and me still there, salvaging, she turned round and said, "Don't forget these," and pelts me, mind, with the four musher-rooms I'd put on her plate. Hit me, too. But I picked them up and I said, "All right, then, all the more for us." So it's war, my boy. Thank God Link hasn't got a atom bomb or he'd drop it for sure.'

'Well, it was his own fault, he gave his notice before I took the job; what the hell's he crying about? Serve him right.'

'Aye, the boy's right enough there, Flossie. He quarrelled with Ben Butch, but he may have been hoping Ben couldn't manage without him.'

'He'd quarrel with God, that one would. But it's not very nice having Nell at my throat, she's bigger than me.'

'If I see her, Mam, I'll tell her to pick on somebody her own size.'

'Job to find one of those, boy; Nell doesn't come in pairs – thank God, too.'

'I won't do any courting sitting here. I'm off. So long. I won't be late.' Joe left his parents in the kitchen, Flossie still in her curlers and her old shabby working clothes.

'Will he marry this one, Floss? She seems a nice little girl.'

'I don't know, mun, he might; and there's a bit of competition about, it might be enough to push him. She may be Miss Right this time.'

'There's been plenty of dud shots before. I wish he'd get married and settle down, I do honest.'

'He will, one of these days. Anything on the telly?'

'There's always something on it, even if it's only those old athletics. How people can sit and watch those beats me, like counting sheep.' They sat on, Flossie trying to summon up the energy to change her clothes and Bryn wishing she'd go so that he could have a go at the paper in peace. Then there was a knock at the back door and Flossie said: 'Who can that be now, I wonder?' She called, 'Come in. Oh, it's you, Steve, come on in out of the wet. Take your mac off. Keeping better?'

'Yes, thanks, Flossie. How's the tubes, Bryn?'

'Tight, boy, tight, but they won't choke me, yet. How's yours? Come for the Death Club, is it?'

'Aye, but there's no hurry, Bryn. I'll sit a minute. Tell me, did Joe go to Ben Butch's today?'

'Yes, he did, indeed; gone out again now though.'

'Everything all right, was it?'

'As far as I know. He didn't complain, did he Flossie?'

'No, glad to be making a bit more money, Joe is, but Nell Link has opened hostilities because he's taken Link's job. Pelted me with musher-rooms today.'

'No?' Steve's good eye registered shocked delight.

'Indeed to God she did. Look, Steve, I haven't changed yet. I'll leave you to talk to Bryn. 'Scuse me a minute, will you, or I'll never get my curlers out? Won't be long. You can have the Death Club when I come down.'

'Yes, right oh, Flossie. I don't know why I keep this old Death Club up, Bryn, indeed. Ideologically it's all wrong, isn't it, now? Welfare State and all, we don't need it any more, but it gives me something to do and it's an excuse to call on people.'

'You don't want no excuse to call on us, whatever, Steve, you know that. How's the children?'

'Fine. All working regular now, except young Sam, of course. Fair play, they're not mean with their money and the missus and me manages all right on the compo. Have a fag?'

'Ta. Joe didn't take much notice of us trying to tell him not to leave the Coal Board, did he? Impetuous, Joe is, impetuous, and you can't really blame the young ones if they want more money, with Take-Over bids and things all over the place.'

'Think Joe's going to make a Take-Over bid for Ben Butch's, Bryn?'

'Joe? Oh, Steve bach, all Joe wants is a motor car to take his girls out in. Young people isn't serious now, not like we used to be. They've had things very easy.'

'Aye.' They were silent for a few moments and looked into the fire, both ageing and disappointed and neither able to draw a decent breath. Flossie came bubbling into the kitchen, her curlers out, the hair rolled and prim; she had a hard blue dress on with a pink pinnie over it. The bright, white china circles of her earrings held her ears out like pot handles. She wore no make-up and her face was gleaming with soap and water; a still-damp dab on the neck of her dress indicated the source of the knock-out smell of lily-of-the-valley that came in with her.

'That was quick work, Flossie, and well worth the trouble. Nice scent you got. I'll have to get some for the missus.'

'Joe gave it to me, from his holiday last year. French it is. Remember, they went on that coach trip to Italy?'

'Jawch, things have changed, haven't they, Bryn boy? Think of colliers going to Italy in our time. Damn, they were lucky to get a week in a tent in Porthcawl or a day down the Mumbles, them days. Many's the time we borrowed a tent when the kids was small and took a bag of food from the Co-op on tick and went for a week to the sands. We enjoyed it too, see. It was a happy time. And now Joe's been to Italy and two of mine have been to France. It's our dreams coming true, see Bryn. I suppose it's a great privilege to see some of your dreams coming true, but it's not the same fun, somehow, the seriousness has gone, hasn't it, mun? There's plenty left to be serious about, only it's like we're afraid to be serious. They wrote plenty of books for us about the social revolution and all that, but nobody can write us a comfortable little tract on how to think about the old Bomb; there's no easy answers in this world no more, Bryn. We haven't got nothing to say, have we?'

'No I expect you're right there, Steve.'

'Steve, don't be so depressing. Put a sock in it, there's a good boy. Here's the shilling for the Death Club, though why I should pay good money for my funeral if I'm going to go up in dust beats me.'

'Thanks, Flossie, let's mark your name off my book. Cheer up, we may all need coffins yet, let's hope, whatever. Well, I'll have to be going on. I don't think I'll bother calling in Link's, somehow – don't feel like anthropology tonight. So long, then, both.'

'So long, Steve, come in again soon; no need to wait for the Death Club, for goodness' sake.'

'Right, then, I will.'

CHAPTER 6

Lil Cream Slices was buying navy blue school knickers from Mrs Griffiths the Stockings.

'Awful hard on her knickers, our Gert is. It's that old gym.'

'Jim? Jim who, in the Man's name?'

'Gym, girl, gymnastics, in school; wears the seat out in a couple of weeks, indeed to God. I'm buying and buying for that girl – well you know yourself, I'm forever in here for something. Education's a great thing, no doubt, but I wish it wasn't so hard on the knickers.' Lil pushed some boxes of stockings to one side and rested her fat, bare arms akimbo on the counter. In her late thirties, Lil had run to fat, her body gone meaningless, like a bundled up feather bed, like a thick evergreen bush, like a sand-dune, but her face was still alive, warmed by her wicked laughter and beady assessment. Her eyes were dark as currants and her hair dyed a tremendous chestnut and permed into bubble curls.

'Give me a pair, Mrs Griffiths; six an'leven, did you say? Put it down, will you, till Friday? Pay you then for sure. Listen, did you hear the latest about old Bill the Chicken Food?'

'Don't tell me he's done something else, Lil. They'll give him jail if he's up again.' Mrs Griffiths the Stockings, Cynthia's mother, was not without her quota of fat, but the steels in her stays were powerful and she was as firm as a tree to the touch. She set her face, pulled it into a look of profound Presbyterian disapproval at the thought of Bill the Chicken Food, but her eyes glinted, nevertheless, and she leaned close towards Lil as she said, in a ladylike hush, 'What is it this time?'

'Well, you know he got that little girl in the way, don't

you, up in Bryncoch Farm? Now, if you please, since her
mother's been telling his history about the place and threatening him with jail – she's only sixteen the girl, see? – he's
been saying in the pubs that the mother can shut up. He says
it's only because she's got better luck than the girl that she's
not in the same boat. He says he was going with the two of
them. One in the barn and the old girl in the parlour. What'd
you think? Isn't he awful? But there's no harm in old Bill,
mind, help anybody if he can, mind.'

'No harm? And that girl only sixteen? He must be forty if
he's a minute. The dirty old pig.'

'Speak as you find, like, isn't it? Did you see the bubble
car down the road last night?'

'No! Gwennie Nightlight's fancy-man?'

'Well, yes, girl, don't you see nothing from this window?
Take a few of those dresses down for you to see some excitement sometimes. You might as well be a sultana in a veil for
all you see through them things. Me and Mrs Morgans Don't
Care was talking, up the street, and we saw the car coming
up, girl, and he parked, see, a few doors from Gwennie's.
Then he came out and passed her door, married man he is,
they say, and he went in the chip shop, to have something to
do, like, I expect, and she must have been watching behind
her parlour curtains. Then, when he comes out again with
this packet of chips, she came out of her door, accidental
done on purpose, you know.'

'Yes,' Mrs Griffiths' eyes were avid now, indecent,
unashamed.

'Mrs Morgans and me went on talking for a bit and
Gwennie stood there talking to him, and the chips must have
been getting stone cold. Dressed up she was, too, in that red
costume of hers.'

'Oh, I know that one all right. I got it for her and she
hasn't finished paying for it yet. She'll be washing the floor
in it before I see all my money, I can tell you.'

'"Well," I said to Mrs Morgans, "she won't go in that bubble car if we're on the road," I said, "you go in and get in the parlour window and I'll hang about a bit to give you time." So in she goes, see, and I pulled a couple of weeds out of my front, round my chrysanths, and then I walks in myself. As soon as my back was turned, girl, Mrs Morgans said, Gwennie nipped into that car and off to go. Emlyn's working nights, of course.'

'Oh, there's a slut, isn't it? And Emlyn such a tidy chap, too.'

'Well, you never know, see, we don't know everything, do we? He may be one of those angels by the road and the devil by the hob for all we know. There's more reasons for things than we can see, sometimes, after all.'

'Why, do you know something about Emlyn, then?'

'No, not I, only speculating, like we do.'

'Who are you speculating about now, Lil? Leave people in peace, both of you, for goodness' sake.' Cynthia pressed into the parlour shop, behind Lil's fortress of a bottom. 'I've got a ladder in these stockings, Mam, can I take another pair?'

There were several lengths of string criss-crossing the shop and Mrs Griffiths had clothes-pegged her selection on them. One line carried silk stockings, hung by their toes, like a bead curtain between the counter and the window, which was blocked out by a row of matronly crêpe dresses on coat hangers, maroon, black, petrol blue and tan, outsize and out-rageous, embroidered and beaded, dateless, dated, and defeated at birth. Diagonally across the shop was a line of handkerchiefs, pegged at the folded corners, like a battleship sending a message. On shelves along the walls were hun-dreds of cardboard boxes with mysterious remarks on them like 'ldys OS Fancy' or 'Wms Ling. 38/40 Pink' and the price in mysterious, secret, Indian-ink letters, ND/V or XW/S, never 3/11 or 4½d., that people could read for themselves and be warned in good time.

Cynthia circumnavigated Lil and ducked under the lines to reach for a pair of stockings. She was pretty, in a dark, monkeyish way. Short, dark, crisp hair, brown eyes, an olive skin and a smile full of strong white teeth. She was short and had to stand on tiptoe to reach her stockings.

'Nice and handy, Cyn, getting a new pair every time you spring a leak. Got a date, is it?'

'Yes, Lil.'

'Same chap I saw you with last week?'

'No, I've made up with Joe Jenkins from Cilhendre again. More homely, like.'

'Oh yes, I know him; better looking really than the other one.'

'Well, I was telling Cyn, Lil, there's no future, is there, in those German boys. Nice enough, no harm in them, they couldn't help it after all, fair play – but it's here today and gone tomorrow, and where are you, isn't it?'

'Yes, that's right enough, Mrs Griffiths. Thinking about going steady, Cyn?'

'She's young enough yet, Lil, have a good time first I always say. Enjoy life while you're young. You're finished, married. She doesn't want to be tied yet.' Mrs Griffiths rearranged the boxes Lil had pushed about the counter and put on her Presbyterian face again and Cynthia, catching Lil's eye under cover of the stockings, winked at her.

'Hey, what time is it, by the way? I mustn't be late or he'll be mad. Masterful type, old Joe.'

Mrs Griffiths looked at the old-fashioned, gold watch on her arm. 'It's nearly seven. Is he coming on the bus?'

'Yes, but I'm as good as ready.' She pulled her new stockings on in the shop, behind the counter, smoothing them over her delicate, well-formed legs with a sensuous caress that the two older women remembered and envied and missed. Lil 'speculated' and Mrs Griffiths was afraid as they watched her, her hair falling, crisp and dark, her body small, slender and vulnerable, her feet and hands neat, trim, controlled. Mrs Griffiths sighed. 'Oh dear, dear,' she breathed.

'What's up with you, Mam?' Cynthia looked up at her mother through the curtain of her hair. 'I wish you wouldn't nag, honest: Joe's a very nice chap, he sings in the chapel, as well.'

'For shame, Cynthia, I didn't say a word out of mouth, did I now, Lil?'

'You don't have to say anything, Mam, that look and that "Oh dear, dear" of yours is enough. And, please,' she threw out her hands, the temper beginning to sharpen in her eyes, 'please, don't say anything about keeping my self-respect. I've heard it before and it's a daft way of saying what you mean. If you've got to say it, say it straight.'

'There's the bus, Cyn, I can hear it.' Lil tidied up the embarrassment. 'Is he coming off, girl? Have a peep through those dresses of your mother's.'

'Yes, there he is. But I won't go out straight away. Bad tactics. He can wait a bit.'

'Nice to be sure like that, isn't it, Mrs Griffiths? I was always the one waiting in my courting days, God help me, too.'

'Won't be long to Christmas now, Lil. I'm starting my Club, if you want to start saving a few shillings.'

'All right, indeed, Mrs Griffiths, I'll take a card Friday, when I pay for these bloomers for our Gert. It'll come in handy no doubt.'

'I've got some lovely scarves on order and a few trinkets – brooches and things. I'm thinking of stocking some Christmas cards as well; no harm in branching out, is there? After all, you've got to pay the bus to get the cheap ones in Swansea, haven't you?'

'Yes, that's right enough. And I've gone too fat now to fight in a crush. Still there, is he, Cyn?'

Cynthia was still standing beside the curtain of crêpe

dresses, watching Joe through a gap in the barricades. She saw him walk around the square and go into the cigarette shop. Then he came out again and stood in the doorway to light a cigarette; he looked nice there like a man in an advertisement, with the light from the shop behind him. Abruptly she picked up her handbag. 'Here goes,' she laughed at them, 'so long.'

'Have a good time, Cyn.'

'Thanks, Lil. So long, Mam.'

'Don't be late, will you, Cyn? So long, then.' When she was safely out of earshot, Mrs Griffiths sighed again. 'Oh dear, dear,' she said.

'She'll be all right, Mrs Griffiths fach, don't worry; you've brought her up lovely, indeed you have.'

She came to meet him in a little confident rush of welcome, her head up, sure, smiling, wide-eyed. She wore a loosely woven tweed suit, peaty brown as her eyes, and a soft silk scarf at her throat in the yellow-greens of mountainsides.

'Hullo, Joe. Been waiting long?'

'No, not too long. You're worth waiting for, anyway. You all right?' Joe's heart had given a positive flick when he saw her coming towards him and his ear was still half-cocked to listen for more reactions.

'Fine, thanks. What shall we do?'

'Let's have a drink, anyway, for a start, is it?'

'Not here anyway, my mother'd be wild. Look, there's the bus, we'll go as far as Pont, no neighbours down there; you can't spit in this place without all the neighbours knowing. Come on, we'll have to run for it. Quick.'

Joe's dignity permitted him to run only on the rugger field, but she belted away from him and ran to the steps of the bus, where she stood and laughed up at the conductor's face. 'Wait a minute, will you, old Joe has to take his time. Ageing fast he is.'

The conductor swung his head round the back of the bus and shouted, 'Hurry along, there, please. Come on, Joe, mun, we're late.' But Joe still took his time and walked at his usual measured speed across the square.

The lounge bar of the Traveller's Rest in Pont was a disheartening sort of place. It had carpets and artificial flowers and a television flicking away in silence in a far corner. It was cold with swank and the few people there looked isolated and lonely, washed-up. Joe sniffed hungrily in the beery direction of the public bar, emancipated from the fetters of carpets and low, glass-topped tables, but Cyn wanted style, and this Joe was prepared to grant, within reasonable limits.

'Nice in here, isn't it?' she said, swallowing the first sip of gin and tonic. 'No rowdies like your old Red Lion.'

'Bit dead though; feels like chapel, you got to talk so quiet. Have a fag.'

'Thanks. When's that gymanfa coming off, Joe? Could I come to hear you singing?'

'Would you come, honest? Would you?'

'When is it, then?'

'Next Sunday, six o'clock in Salem.'

'All right, then, I will.'

'And wait for me after, is it? Flossie'll be there, she'll want you to come home for supper. Would you be willing?'

'O.K., I don't mind. That's fixed, then; I'll see you outside the chapel, is it?'

'Yes, by the second gravestone on the right.'

'Why that one? Any reason?'

'He's my grandfather. Nice old boy, he'd like a look at you.'

'Why?'

'You know why. Don't fish.'

'Spite. What are you drinking, anyway?'

'Export. Have a swig, it's nice. Go on, taste it.'

'No, they might see me.'

'Go on, don't be daft, nobody's looking. They're all too busy looking at your legs, anyway, to bother what you're doing.'

'Quick, then. Not bad.'

'Have half a pint after that gin?' Joe wasn't at ease in this pub. Those bloody waiters in their white coats looking down their noses at a chap's hands. Think a bloke's got no right in here because he works underground – colour-bar in Pont, myn uffern i, colliers is black, look down your bloody nose. But I'll have more in my pay-packet than you, boyo, come you. He jerked his head at one of them. 'Another pint, son, and bring us a half as well.' I'll tip this snotty bastard now, that'll shake him. And look at his shoes, for God's sake, round toes and patches – he can do with a tip, too, by the looks of him. How will Export go down on top of gin, mun?

'Generous tonight, Joe.'

'Oh, well, they don't get much, these blokes, do they?'

'How's the new job going?'

'All right, so far. More money, whatever.'

'We're not getting much coal in Number 4. There's been rumours that they're thinking of closing it.'

'Be out of a job then, will you?'

'Yes, have to go on the dole, unless I can find somebody to keep me.'

'That shouldn't be very hard.' Joe, here's you chance, mun; say something, it's an invite, mun, go on. 'Been seeing that German lately?' Her face closed and he could have bitten his tongue out.

'I see him in work every day. He always looks in to see how I am.'

'Nice of him.'

'Well, he is nice, so there. He's got nice manners, what-ever.'

'And I haven't, I suppose.'

'If the cap fits, you can wear it, boyo. Oh, don't be childish, Joe, I've been looking forward to tonight, honest. Germans are nice enough, but not homely, not comfortable, you're always in your best clothes with them, you know? Well, now, what'll we do? There's a good picture on here, would you like that?'

'Whatever you say. All right, if we can sit in the back row.'

'One-track mind you've got, Joe Jenkins.'

'Can you blame me, with you about the place? Every man in this pub would give a week's wages to be where I am now.'

'You can be nice when you try, can't you.'

'Just give me a chance, ducks. Come on, then, if we're going.'

They sat in the back row in the cinema among the other lovers. Joe hardly looked at the screen, but felt he'd had his money's worth, none the less. They left the place in a laughing, bubbling, foolish, fooling mood of lightly veiled desire, not yet localised or pressing.

'Let's have another drink, is it, Cyn, before they close. Want to go back to that posh old place?'

'Oh, yes, please, Joe. I might see somebody I know, that I could show off to. Are you willing?'

'O.K., if you say so.' He took her hand, and slipped it, warm as a mouse, into his trousers pocket.

'It'll have warmed up there now, you'll see.'

'I'm warmed up enough. A bit of quiet I want now, to cool off. There's nowhere quiet in this bloody place, is there? Will your mother be in tonight?'

'Yes, Joe Jenkins, she will. Don't get any ideas.'

'No harm in thinking, is there?'

'Depends what you think, my boy.'

'Like you said, one-track mind.' He opened out her little fisted hand in his pocket and pressed her fingers into his groin.

'Oh, Joe, you're awful, honest; where were you brought up?'

'Flossie brought me up, bless her – but you will come Sunday, won't you? Promise?'

'Yes, I'll come. Will she put out her best supper cloth for me?'

'She'll even have the Shelley China out of the cabinet, if I tip her the wink. There'll be a spread, give old Floss half a chance. And Cyn – you know about my father's nose, don't you? It's a bit on the long side, so be prepared. Flossie makes jokes about it, to pretend she doesn't care; a bone of contention the old man's nose is.'

'Well, you haven't got it, anyway, and it's your nose I care about.'

'Do you care about it?'

'Of course I do, dope. Here we are, I hope there's somebody I know in here.'

'Look, I want to go to the Gents first. Go to the lounge, is it, and I'll be in as fast as I can.'

'O.K., Joe, but don't take all night.' Cynthia walked confidently away through the carpets, her hair rich and bouncy, her head up, and Joe watched her: you've fallen, Joe boy, this is it all right. She's bloody marvellous, mun, look at her; the old man would like her, too – who wouldn't, worse luck? He turned towards the Gents. My car money would have to go if we went steady, but at least I've got that much and old Mam would help out.

When Joe got to the lounge bar he couldn't see Cynthia; then, in a great gust of over-loud laughter near the bar, he heard a high-pitched voice say, precisely, 'To Cynthia,' and there she was in the middle of them and all of them holding up their glasses to her and saying 'Cynthia'. She was loving it and Joe could have killed her. She didn't see him, blinded as she was with popularity and attention, and he went white with a rage that drew his face like an illness. He walked, still

slowly and measured, up to where she stood, pushing his way
to her. 'I thought you were supposed to be out with me.
Who's it to be? Me or them?' He talked through his teeth and
crushed her arm in his big hand. He stared into her face,
wanting to smash it for a mad red moment as he watched her
expressions change. The first flick was outrage and then an
almost obscene look of delight took over and she licked her
lips, her eyes bright, like a woman in a boxing match, and
then she jerked, remembering her manners. 'Joe,' she said
firmly, like a school teacher, 'I want you to meet my German
friends from the colliery.' Her expression changed again and
her eyes were begging him now to back her up like Flossie
when he was cheeky in front of somebody. 'They've bought
us drinks; look, there's your Export all ready for you.' She
turned away from him, tiny among the men, but dominating
them. 'This is Joe Jenkins,' she said, 'the one I told you
about, who sings so well.'

Boorishly Joe looked at them, his face still white, his nostrils flared and his jaw aggressive. 'Hullo,' he said. Then, in
turn, each of the Germans said his own name and clicked his
heels: 'Winkelmann', 'Sprotte', 'Müller', 'Gronemann',
'Lietke', 'Willgerodt'.

'Hullo,' Joe said again, wondering which was the one. She
picked up his drink from the bar. 'Here you are, Joe, here's
your Export.'

'Ta,' he said while the refrain 'Bloody Nazis, bloody
Nazis' kept whipping up the fury in his brain. Then one of
them offered him a cigarette. 'Do you smoke? It does not
harm your throat?'

'Thanks,' his big rough hands were clumsy as he fumbled
the cigarette from the packet, but the hand that held the
packet was a worker's hand too and the sight of that work-
shaped hand, battered like his own, made him look up into
the man's face and he saw a little insignificant, back-bent,
greasy, black-haired man with a broken nose and pleading

brown eyes. His anger slowly thawed, the ugly grip around his throat eased. He looked more like a Nazi himself than this chap did. She was saying that they'd been to the pictures and what a good film it had been.

'Liar,' he said, his voice now under control, quiet, bantering, claiming, 'you had your eyes closed most of the time. You didn't see a quarter of it.'

She looked like a kitten among them and they all laughed at her and she blushed and giggled. From the public bar they heard singing and gusts of beery laughter. 'She'll be coming round the mountain when she comes, she'll be wearing silk pyjamas when she comes . . .' One of the Germans – Joe had no idea which was which – said, 'Why do we drink in here while next door they sing?'

She turned to Joe. 'It's all right by me. What about you, Joe? Shall we go?' He relished the half-humble look she gave him. 'Aye, I'll come. Anywhere out of this. But let me stand my round first. Same again, is it?'

He stayed close to her, holding her arm, as they went through to the warm, thick, friendly atmosphere of the public bar. One of the Germans went up to the piano. He was small, with a sad face, full of lines and big grey eyes. 'You will sing, please?' he said, turning his face up at Joe.

'What solo are you going to sing on Sunday, Joe? Perhaps he knows that one.'

'Handel it is, from *The Messiah*.'

'Ah, then I know, indeed.'

'"Comfort ye", then.'

'Good.' He shrugged his shoulders. 'But this old piano, you know, it is not much for music, you will forgive me.'

Joe put his pint down on the top of the old, drunken, walnut piano, still a bit sulky, but grim too, determined to show them something. The pub was hardly the place for chapel music, but he'd practised it and they'd get it, damn them. The talkers in the bar fell silent as the pianist played the opening chords and then Joe's great voice sang 'Comfort ye', and then 'Comfort ye, my people' spread out over the smell of beer and the spit and the tired miners and the few old women and Cyn and the Germans, and Joe forgot them and was simply singing, oblivious to his audience and the anger and the crouching, instinctive male antipathy.

He finished and took up his pint, drinking in the shouts of 'Encore' and the pride of possession in Cynthia's eyes. The drinkers stamped and somebody called for another round and they all sang 'Pack up your troubles' and 'Lily Marlene' and friendly feeling gushed about, as honest as in-laws at a wedding. The mood was shallow, sentimental, drunken, dishonest, and everybody was happy and a little row of pints was set up on the piano for Joe. When time was called Joe was drunk with praise and pints and all the Germans came together to see the two of them off on the bus, with cameraderie and compliments flying.

'Now then, I told you they were decent chaps, didn't I? Nothing wrong with them, was there, Joe?'

'Not so bad, love, not so bad. Old Joe showed them, didn't he?'

'You were lovely, honest; but weren't you mad when you first came in? You were awful, mind.'

'Was I? What did I do, then?'

'Went white for a start and shouted at me and pulled my arm and everything.'

'Serve you right. What did I do then?'

'I thought you were going to fight them all till you saw your pint all ready and then you took it and remembered your manners and said "Ta".'

'Was I a disgrace, then?'

'No. Shall I tell you something? I loved it, seeing you so mad about me, it was nice in an exciting sort of way. Oh, Joe, I think I'm a bit drunk.'

'Good. Are we friends, then?'

'Of course we are.'

'Can I come in to your house tonight?'

'Not tonight, Joe, you smell of beer and my mother'd be mad if she thought you took me to pubs.'

'Where shall we go, then, Cyn? I must have a bit of peace and quiet in the dark before I go.' Joe, boy, it's no good, with all that beer you're carrying you'd get nowhere, boy, nowhere. You're loaded, boy, loaded; don't try anything, you might let yourself down. Who, me? Ever know me fail? But with the load you're carrying, lad.

'Cyn, which was the one, you know, the one took you out?'

'Oh, that one, he's the one played the piano.'

'That one? I could put him in my waistcoat pocket, mun. What did he do? Take a chair out with him?'

'There's no need to be so nasty, Joe Jenkins, he's very nice and he's lonely and far from home. There's no harm.'

'Cyn, will you go out with him again?'

'What's it to you, Joe Jenkins?'

'You know all right. I like you, see, and I've asked you to supper haven't I?'

'Is that supposed to mean something, then?'

'Yes.'

'What?'

'Oh, you know, for God's sake. Want it in writing?'

'No, I want it in words though.'

'Well, love, you've come to the wrong shop, Jenkins isn't very strong on the words; actions, I like. Where can we go, mun, Cyn?'

'You'll have to wait till Sunday, boy.'

'Promise? I'll get Flossie to light a fire in the front room. Don't forget you promised, now.'

'Take it easy, I didn't say what I was promising, did I?'

'I didn't need it in words, ducks, all I need is the little green light.' Then, like a man stepping on his own corns he said, 'Did that pianist chap put it in words?'

She giggled, gave a little drunken snort down her nose, 'Don't say if I tell you, will you? Know what he did mostly, said poetry in German and translated it to me. He taught me one bit in German.

"Du schlank und rein wie eine Flamme
Du wie der Morgen zart und licht
Du blühend Reis vom edlen Stamme
Du wie ein Quell geheim und schlicht."

That means, "You, slim and clean like a flame, you like morning, soft and light, you, flower from a noble stem, you like a source, simple and secret." Pretty isn't it? Very romantic anyway, not like you, old Joe.'

'You like that, do you? All right, I'll say Welsh poetry to you. I like poetry, too, you know that? Hey, I must be drunk, it's always a sign, if I say I like poetry. I keep it dark when I'm sober.'

'O.K. I'll keep you drunk. Come on, here's the stop.'

Joe was yanked out of his glass-cage world of frothy content and self-esteem as he walked, jaunty as a bantam rooster, home from his bus. As he came, top of the beery world, down Railway Street, three figures who had been leaning, smoking, against an electric light pole came towards him and stood in his path, barring his way. He couldn't see them properly, with their backs to the light, and their stopping him was so melodramatic and extraordinary that he felt a gulp of fear for a minute.

One of them said, 'You Joe Jenkins?'

'Yes, I am. Want anything, then?'

'Want to give you a bit of advice, boyo. Keep away from my sister, if you know what's good for you.'

'What the hell are you talking about? I don't know your sister. Don't know you either – stand in the light for a chap to have a look at you.'

'You know my sister all right. I've been tipped off. Sall's husband may have left her, but he's still keeping her. If it comes to his ears Sall's going out with others, he won't have to pay no more. That's the law; a man need not support an adulterous wife, we had it from the lawyer, and how's she going to live, then? You won't keep her.' The taller figure, the spokesman, moved and the street light fell on the face of one of the others.

'Good God, you're not Sall's brothers? I've seen you before, I remember now. Don't you play for Ammanford? Played against you, haven't I?'

'Look, we're not interested in who you've played against, it's the fun and games with Sall we're talking about. Stop it, see? Put a sock in it or we'll stop you. I may be a bit old, but my pals by here can fix you. We're giving you fair warning and there's three of us. We'll give you such a hiding you won't forget and you won't be much good to Sall or anybody else when we've finished. See? Bear it in mind, boy, bear it in mind.'

'Who the hell d'you think you are, dictating to me? Are you Sall's jailers or what? If I see Sall and she comes out with me none of you's going to interfere, and you can keep your bloody noses out of my business; what's between Sall and me is our affair and you can bugger off.'

'You asked for it, boy, don't blame us,' and, like a shot from a film, like Chicago, like Sall's paper books, the shorter one, the footballer, gave Joe a quick clip on the jaw and, as he rocked on his drunken balance, the other young one came in with two heavy ones to the pit of his stomach. Then they touched their slouch hats, which had stayed put throughout all the randybo, and said, 'Good night, now, and don't forget. That's only a taste.'

Joe was propping himself up against the gate-post of 'The Court Where the Nightingale Sings', feeling the pain like a blush run through him, aware of the roughness of brick under his hand, dazed with beer and blows. He was madly angry, but the men had gone, and suddenly all the beer came up to his mouth and down his nose and he was helplessly sick all over the pavement.

CHAPTER 7

Dai Dialectic called for Joe next morning in his ramtishackle old 1938 Austin. The car smelt of coal and underground and was very noisy, but it went like a bird and had only cost sixteen pounds when Dai bought it. Krem sat beside Dai in the front and Joe had the back seat to himself. Dai got into gear, like a cowboy on a bucking bronco.

'Been in the wars, Joe?' Krem eyed Joe's jaw with an appreciative, sly assessment.

'Aye.' Joe was non-committal.

'Who hit you, boy? Not Steve, was it, for coming in with us?'

'No; poor old Steve, he hasn't got the wind for a punch any more.'

'You caught a fourpenny one there, all right.'

Joe's shame at his bashing was fighting with his indignation at the unfairness of the contest. The indignation won. 'I got attacked, mun, indeed to God – here in Cilhendre, mind. Place is coming to something.'

'No! Drop dead?'

'Aye, I was coming home last night, mun, been out with Cyn – you know, Cyn Griffiths.' The thought of Cyn helped his pride along. 'Came off the last bus, see, and these chaps were waiting for me by the top of the street. I didn't know the buggers, three of them it was. And they came up, mun, and told me to lay off Sall – Sall Ever Open Door, you know. Or else, they said. One of them said he was her brother. I told them where they got off and to mind their own, and, damn, if the two young ones didn't pitch into me before I knew where I was, and then they jumped into this car they had and beat it. But I'll get them yet, come you; they picked the wrong boy, they did. First chance I get I'll take old Sall out, give her the works and be ready for them. No one's dictating to this boy.'

'Why the hell did they pick on you then, Joe? Sall's had plenty of others, God knows.'

'P'raps they're taking us in turns, like Sall, bless her. They said if her husband came to hear about her carrying on he wouldn't pay for her no more, the lawyer said he doesn't have to; that's what they said.'

'Oh.' Krem was trying vainly to think how different the law was in Russia.

'There's no need to talk about this up there, boys; once I get a bit of dirt on it they won't notice. I don't want Cyn to know, she'd play hell, honest. And you know what an old nanny-goat Cyril Toupee is, he'll have it all over the bloody valley in two minutes.'

'O.K., mum's the word by here. Why don't you wipe your face with your cap now, put a bit of camouflage on, like? Aye, go on, cover it; you can say you got dirty in this old car of Dai's, isn't it, Dai?'

'Aye, aye, there's enough coal in this car to start a small mine by itself, indeed to God. The missus don't half complain; swears she's getting silicosis in the back seat.'

'Fancy those chaps doing that, though. You ought to have reported them to the cops by right, Joe.'

'Don't be daft, mun, Krem, where's your sense?'

'Use your loaf, Krem, the boy doesn't want his girl to know he went with Sall; girls don't understand, mun. Think of your old woman.'

'No thanks, I rather not, first thing in the morning. Nice girl, is she, Joe?'

'Aye, she's not bad indeed; pretty smashing, Krem.'

'Make the most of it, boy, make the most of it. They all gets old in time.'

'Aye, old and mean with it. I wonder what she's put in

my sandwiches today. I've had bloody tomatoes till I'm sprouting.'

'P'raps she's given you caviar, Krem.'

'What hopes, in this bloody country?'

'Ever tasted it?'

'No, not I. Don't know what it looks like, to tell the truth.'

'Somebody told me it looks like black jam and tastes of fish.'

'Honest, Joe?'

'Aye, so they say, anyway.'

'The Russian working-man eats it every day.'

'Fish jam every day? Worse than tomatoes every day, Krem.'

'But they like it, see, it's one of their treats.'

'You can't account for tastes, can you?'

The car went on through the early morning, past buses full of clean, N.C.B. colliers, past the silent school, past the Co-op with the blinds down on self-service, past the sleeping pub, the prowling cats, the dust-bins, the dark houses where the women had gone back to bed; it was a man's world, a world of working working-men; grocers, preachers, teachers, typists had no place in it, bowler hats and umbrellas, over-shoes and ties would take over only when the salt of the earth had gone down, down to the darkness and the flickering lights and the fellow-feeling and the jokes, with the dripping water and the rats and the killing dust.

They turned off the main road and the little car pounced and jiggered over the mountain dirt-road. On the lower slopes, the brown bracken was dank and dishevelled and dilapidated; a few silly, out-of-step flowers still hung about on the red stalks of the brambles and the sage spikes of the gorse bushes were still defiant, but their yellow bursts of flowers were now wet, bedraggled, dark brown pods. The leaves were all off the thin elder trees, and the little oaks seemed to lie close and tight, gathered in against the threat.

The road climbed, past the skeleton whinberry bushes and on, through the rough, crisp, fawn-coloured grass, till the grass made way for the small coal and the black mud.

Dai parked his car near the bottom of the chute, where Cyril had already backed his lorry to wait for the first tram loads that he would drive to Cardiff, to Margam, to the corners of the Principality. They walked up to the top, took their lamps from the office and stood with their hands raised like captured crooks while Ben Butch frisked them for their cigarettes and matches. Joe, his dirty face unremarkable in that place of dirt, lit his safety lamp and Ben tested it, blowing a long breath all around it.

One by one the men assembled: twelve colliers, Joe, Ben Butch and Cyril the Lorry. Joe went down first to test the air with his lamp and Cyril Toupee, his transformation safely in his coat pocket, lumbered off with Krem to the pasture above the drift to catch the little grey colliery horses, strong, patient, willing and fearless of the below-ground dark. The men talked to the horses, fondling them, making up to them, while they waited for Joe's shout that the air was clear; then they too went down and Joe came back to the office to organise the day with Ben.

'Right, then, that's clear enough. But listen, Joe, I'm well behind on my allocation this week, with being without a fireman and that. You couldn't come in and blow a few holes Sunday, could you? We'd have the way clear then to get on first thing Monday morning. You'd have a clear road Sunday, with the boys out.'

'Oh, I don't know about this Sunday, Ben – I'm singing, see, in Salem gymanfa. I couldn't let Fred the Singing down, not now. The programmes are out and all.'

'Not singing all day, mun, are you?'

'No, only in the night, actually.'

'Well, what's to stop you coming up for an hour or two in the day? Be a big help to me, honest, and I'll see you right. Double-time for Sunday – you want the money, don't you?'

'I could do with the cash, for a fact.'

'Well, come in, then, will you, boy? I'd appreciate it, indeed to God I would. The boys want to fill the trams, too, see, they'd all be grateful; they were short last week too, like me.'

'All right, then, I'll come up in the morning. If we do the boring Saturday, I wouldn't be long firing Sunday morning.'

'Thanks, Joe, you're a pal; I'll see you right, never fear.'

CHAPTER 8

There was pandemonium in all the chapel houses on Sunday morning. Steve's was no exception.

'Have you cleaned my best shoes?'

'Where's that white collar I bought last week? If somebody's got it on . . .'

'Damn this cat, she's slept in my slouch.'

'You eat your egg before you put on that tie. I haven't got time to sponge you down today.'

'Give us a go with the clothes brush, will you? This is the last time anybody's bringing a bloody white cat to this house. Look at my hat, mun.'

'Spit on the brush, then.'

'What you doing to my cat?'

'Putting it out – under my feet by here and sleeping in my best hat.'

'Where's the black-currant jam? I got a sore throat now.'

'Serve you right, shouting about the place like that. It isn't my fault you used the black brush on your brown shoes. Here, Steve, give me that hat. Oh, I can't breathe in this new corset.'

'Take it off then, for God's sake.'

'Couldn't get my skirt on without it. Can't button it as it is. Like my hat?'

'You look like Napoleon, honest – after Waterloo.'

'You can't say anything, Lord Nelson. Sam, that's the last bit of black-currant jam I've got. Leave it be. Hey, mind my skirt, will you? Wash those hands before you touch anything else, Sam.'

'Sam, boy, go out, will you? There's no room in this kitchen for you, your brothers and your mother's behind.'

'Can I go out, our Mam?'

'Oh, all right, go on; but you come back early for dinner, mind, and don't forget it's Sunday.'

'Can I take my cart?'

'No, I told you, it's Sunday.'

'I want to take my cart. Dad, I want to take my cart.'

'You heard your mother. Go on, get out, go for a walk, go for a picnic, go somewhere, only go.'

Since his father had instructed him to go for a picnic, Sam grabbed a packet of biscuits behind his mother's bustling back and went to round up his friends. Wilf produced the savings for the auditors' inspection and they trailed once more to the Italian's shop, to calculate how to spend their money all over again. But it was Sunday morning, even for the Italian, and his window was blind. The unnatural, still quiet of Sunday morning was like a weary load on their backs; half-heartedly they skited a tin or two into the river until an early deacon copped them and threatened to tell their fathers.

'Oh, let's get out of this.' Sam put his now empty biscuit bag on his head. 'Come on, I'm Gagarin in my space hat. We'll play Japs and Yanks up the mountain.'

'Well, I'm not being the Jap again, so there,' Wilf protested.

'But you're the smallest, you got to be.'

'Well, I'm not coming, then.'

'Come on, mun Wilf, you can be the Jap sniper up a tree. Geraint will lend you his glasses, won't you, Ger?'

'O.K. Aye, only don't break them, or I'll cop it.'

Wilf took the specs, pulled his hair down in a fringe and went *Chrrrr*, pointing a Sten gun at them; then they ducked behind the garden hedges and stole the last bits of summer for camouflage. They stalked a jungle tiger up the mountain, bracken and brambles and gorse bushes grown tall and menacing, with a boa-constrictor in every branch and poisonous jumping spiders ready to pounce at every ambush.

Wilf, flat on his belly, lay deep behind a forest of brown bracken stalks, plaited together by a domineering, triumphant bramble that had thrown great thick spars, arching and smooth, above his head. At the bottom, the stalks were all brown and naked and the first, brown-powdered fronds of the bracken were curled in, crimped, like rusty tin, like a part of a grabbing space-machine; the top ones were still green, the top of the world was green. A few missed blackberries were mouldy and lingering, whiskered and grey above his head as he pulled the rust-brown seeds off a dock into his fist and felt their crispness slip through his fingers. He could watch the world through the stalks, the clear world of Geraint's glasses. He had the world in his sights. He was watching for the Yanks, easing his Sten, adjusting his camouflage, when he saw a man come quickly towards him. The man was part of the jungle, that he should pause and look around and seem to be watchful was only proper, fitting, jungle behaviour. Wilf kept him in his sights as he moved, came closer, and Wilf would have gone *Chrrrr* at him, but he saw that the man was Link dressed up for Sunday, and no friend to children. Wilf crouched deeper behind his tangle as Link passed, let him pass without his money or his life or as much as the password. His going brought them all out of hiding.

'See old Link, then?'

'Where's he going? Off to visit his relations p'raps.'

Geraint crouched down from his shoulders, bent his knees out, and scratched himself under the armpit.

'Who was he playing lickalockie with? See him dodging round the trees?'

'P'raps his relations didn't want him to come, p'raps they hate him.' Geraint lifted back his head and let out a howl of anthropoid agony and proceeded to walk in a circle like a demented gorilla, then the others followed his example till Geraint decided to turn nasty and attacked Sam with teeth bared. Wilf, being a bit small, decided that gorilla fights were not for him and started a little fire on his own, with Sam's biscuit bag, a gorse bush and some of his store of stolen matches. The gorse set up a satisfying crackle and then a roar and they all rushed like lunatics to find more and more and more fuel. Then Wilf, ordering and bossing his fire, burned his hand and cried and the tears ran over his smoky face and he rubbed them away with gorse-black hands. 'I'm going home,' he said. 'We've got to go to the gymanfa after dinner and look at the colour of us. Anybody got a hankie?'

'No.'

'Our Mam won't half give me it, black on a Sunday. I had a bath last night ready for the singing.'

'What the hell have you got to complain about? I got a burn, she'll know I been playing with fire and she said she'll tell my father the next time.'

'Well, don't show her the burn, hide it.'

''S hurtin' though.'

'Close your fist and put your hand in your pocket and put ointment on it on the sly. She'll never know, she'll be too busy today, getting you all ready for the singing.'

'Well, come on home then, I'm fed up. Bloody silly old fire of hell. I'm off. Hope it's going to rain.'

'Hey, we can't leave this fire like this, can we?'

'I can, I'm going.'

'Hey, no, Wilf, come back. I got an idea. We'll all pee on it, to spite it for burning you, and that'll put it out. Come on, let him have it. All together. One, two, three, go.'

Link was on his way up to see the horses. Not for the world would he let anyone know where he was going, that he missed the company of those old horses in Brynhyfryd. He had passed the hidden children and gone on, up past the drift, and up to the pasture beyond. He went down to the far corner of the field, out of sight, down the far side, where, in a hollow, alders grew and there was fresh water. He called

them to him, gave them the bits of apples he had in his
pockets for them, browned and gritty and garnished with
wisps of tobacco and fluff.

'Hullo, then,' he said. 'Been missing old Tom, have you?
Nobody looking after you proper, now, is there, lovies? How
are you, Bluebell fach, all right, is it? Well, well, you don't
look too good, Thunder, my boy. Got a cut on your back,
have you? – ych y fi, the old flies are troubling you. Never
mind, Tom will put some Archangel Tar on it tonight. I'll
come back to see you tonight and we'll soon fix that old cut.
Listen, Tom's got a new job now, down in Cwmtwrch, but he
won't forget you. He'll come and see you, honest, now.' He
took a curry comb from his pocket and began to groom the
horses, talking, talking to them the while.

Joe slept late on Sunday. His mother hadn't the heart to wake
him from his deep, abandoned sleep, on the one morning of
the week that was his own. She was angry that he had promised to go to work that day, and she left him to sleep when
she and Bryn went off to the morning service. When she
came back from chapel, in her shocking pink suit and flowered hat, Joe was up and dressed in his working clothes with,
as Flossie said the skin of his bum on his brow.

'Why the hell didn't you call me, Mam? Look at the time.
I'm not waiting for dinner, I got to go.'

'You were tired, boy; an hour or two won't make all that
difference; you said it was only a small job, didn't you?
Look, the meat's ready, you have a bit of that; wait now, let
me take off my hat, whatever. Where's my pinnie? Here,
Bryn, cut him a few slices off the leg and I'll cut some bread
and butter. Don't tramp about like something in a cage, our
Joe, it won't be a minute.'

'I haven't got a minute, I tell you. I'm off.'

'Joe Jenkins, you're not going out of this house on an
empty stomach, so you can stop your antics and sit down.

There you are, now pitch in and eat that. Only take you five minutes with your old wolf eating and you'll be glad of it later on. Come on, now, there's a good boy.'

'Oh, all right again. Come on then, let's have it. Got a drop of sauce, or something?'

'There it is, in front of you; want something to take with you?'

'No, I'll be back. Put my clean clothes ready, will you, and keep up the fire for water, whatever you do. I can't sing black.'

'Yes, yes, all right. You don't have to tell me, for goodness' sake. Pitch in now, boy.'

'Why the hell you didn't call me beats me, honest. I hate rushing like this; I'll be singing breathless, you watch.'

'I'm sorry, love, but you need the rest, out to the world you were.'

'I told you enough, Flossie; I knew he'd be mad.'

'I need the time more today. Well, I'm off. Be back as soon as I can. So long.'

'Take care of yourself, bach.'

'So long, boy.'

''Bye.' He pulled on his old broken-nosed working cap, glistening with coal-dust in the October sunshine. At the door, he turned, looking defenceless and little again. 'Mam, you haven't forgotten about Cyn coming, have you?'

'Don't be soft. I got a spread ready, the pantry looks like Salem Social.'

'Thanks, mun, Mam. See you, then.' He hurried as hard as his out-of-doors dignity would allow up the garden path and out through the back gate to the short-cut to the mountain. His thoughts had scattered in the morning rush, like starlings routed by a dog, but as he walked with long, easy strides towards the mine, the feel of Sunday and the open mountain and the warm quiescent excitement for Cynthia pulled him together again. Get this little job done now, Joe, have a bath and half an hour to practise; hope I'm good tonight; fair play, old Fred has worked hard. I wonder what she'll be wearing? I like her in that brown thing. Fair play to old Flossie too; let's hope she remembers to light the parlour fire. If Flossie mentions that fight absent-minded, I'll slay her. What the hell could I tell Cyn if she found out? Christ, she wouldn't half be mad. I don't think she'll notice this bruise by now. Good Lord, what's that? I'm sure it's a fox, yes it is, it is; hard to see against the bracken, but it's a fox all right – well, I'll be damned, just like that poem. That was on a Sunday too, the bells of the church calling us to service and the something something calling to the mountain. There he goes, he's seen me, yes, that's right too, that's how he went, like the poem; it happened, finished, like a falling star. Wouldn't mind if I'd written that myself. Better than singing. Oh, I don't know, too. I like singing and it suits me better. Watch old Joe spouting poetry round the pubs; God, I can just see a few of those drinkers if Jenkins suddenly started saying poems about the place. No, poetry is a secret thing. Got to keep it dark, but if you sing the poem it's all right. Funny thing, I hope I can do this job quickly now and get back. Flossie was a nit to let me sleep on like that. I could be finished now. I hope those bastards aren't hard on old Sall; I wouldn't like to get her into trouble, she's a decent sort. But there's others beside me; why pick on me, for God's sake? I can't see why Cyn should come to hear of it. Unless they told her. Would they? Might be better if I told her myself. Be a bit hard to explain after the way I carried on about that German. I won't spoil tonight, whatever, roll on suppertime.

Joe heard the sudden *Chrrrr* of a sub-machine gun, put up his hands in surrender and was ordered to hand over his money or his wife. 'You've had all my money, you devils. Still got it safe?'

'Show it, Wilf.'

'Here it is, Joe, look; we lost a shilling. Old Fatty Wilks

stole it, but the master gave us one back instead. Our Mam has promised me two and a tanner, if I'm good from now till Guy Fawkes.'

'Any hopes, Wilf?' Joe went over to brush bits of autumn off Wilf's lumber-jacket.

'As long as she doesn't find nothing out, like.' Wilf stuffed his burned hand deep into his trousers pocket.

'My grannie said I can have her supplementary pension – two and 'leven – if I do all her messages till Christmas. Old shark my grannie is – till Christmas, mind.'

'P'raps she'll die before Christmas. People's grannies are always dying about the place.'

'Mine won't, she's only just had a new perm.'

'Looking smart now, is she, Geraint? Why is Wilf wearing your glasses, then, Ger?'

'He's the Jap, see?'

'Oh, yes. Well, so long, partners, I got to get cracking.'

'Working overtime, is it, Joe?'

'Aye, your mothers will have to put in a bit of overtime on you lot too, if you're going to the singing. It's late, you know that? You'll cop it if you don't belt home.'

'On our way, brother, on our way. Be seeing you.'

'So long, then.'

'So long, Joe, boy.'

Joe gave them his chopped off salute, they presented arms and marched off in single file, shouting into the Sunday quiet, 'Ask your mother for sixpence . . .' while he jerked up the climb of the mountain along the sheep track in the tussocky, fawn grass, till his track joined the coal-dirt road that Ben Butch had worked for his lorries.

There's a mess old Ben's made up here with his workings. He's spoilt the look of the mountain altogether. Will he have to tidy it up when he's got all the coal out, I wonder? God, it's quiet up here. There isn't even a bird out. You brushed the autumn from my coat – that's not a bad first line there, Joe.

You brushed the autumn from my coat – we'll say it was Cyn, not old Wilf – from my coat, your hands were something on my wintered thighs. Come on Joe, you're doing fine, your hands were summer on my wintered thighs, no that's pushing it too hard. Old Cilhendre looks nice down there. They'll have a job getting Wilf and those clean; I wouldn't have minded hearing the kids this afternoon, I like to see them up on the gallery, scrubbed and slicked; they look so damn daft all pansied up, when you know they're proper beatniks underneath the wash-and-brush-up.

He came to the top of the last sharp rise, to the mouth of the silent drift; the place was desolate, comfortless, no fire in the brazier, no sign of horses, no shouts, no flickering friendly lights. He unlocked the dilapidated office door and the slam of its opening rattled the whole ramshackle structure, rattled the silence. He stood in the doorway and looked about him, tall, silhouetted against the bright October. His steel helmet was hanging there, with the lamp and the flat, American-army green, weighty battery. He put the hat on his head, wobbling a bit of comfort into it, and hung his old tweed cap in its place. He fixed the battery on to his leather belt and then lit his safety lamp. He put his cigarettes and matches down beside the telephone, and, crouching on his haunches, he unlocked the cupboard on which the telephone stood and gathered together all the gear he would need to fire the holes: detonator, gelignite, the battery, fuses; he checked them over carefully, conscientiously, with the collier's inbred respect for the forces of malignant nature.

He carried the heavy burden out into the sunlight again. The silence was still and heavy about him, the utter quiet got on his nerves. God, it's quiet up here. It's like being kept in after school. I wish I had a bit of company, no mistake. What's the matter with you, Joe, you're talking like a kid? There was a journey of six trams full of coal at the mouth of the drift, waiting for Cyril Toupee on Monday; they stood on the rails where the horses had left them. As Joe passed them, he kicked the sprags which held them safe, to check that each was firm, and then he passed by, into the darkness ahead.

He shivered in the sudden chill of the dripping dark after the warm sun. Strikes cold in here after walking, seems worse because there's nobody about. He hurried down the first incline, stooping low, for the roof in Ben's mine was as inconsistent as the rolling land above; the coal had ducked and jerked about in places, like a worm in turned earth. The water swirled about his feet and his lights caught the diamond dripping. His coming alerted the rats and their little scurryings splashed ahead of him.

It was an untidy place. On top of the utter absence of comfort there was an irritating, unnecessary, inhuman clutter about: discarded links of giant chain, pasted with coal-mud, ends of props thrown aside, a pick propped almost elegantly against the coal wall, horse droppings, spit, a dead rat. It grew hotter as he travelled down to the headings, his burden was heavy and he could have done with a cigarette. He paused, where the roof was high enough, to stretch his backbone and throw his head back. He bit a chew off his plug tobacco and spat at the two eyes of a rat that winked in his light. He came to the borings he had already made and set in his first firings. As he rammed home the plug, his light caught a flash of white quartz in the granite wall and he touched it gently, as though to apologize that he would have to destroy it, as though to say good-bye to it.

Alone, wrapped around by the heat, the damp, the dark, the quiet, he was aware of his nerves in his finger-tips and in the bottom of his stomach; slightly sickened by the taste of chewed tobacco, his teeth and lips gritty, and the smell of explosive filling his lungs; his back and the backs of his legs ached with stooping and crawling and his feet were paddling in the warm, black water that had seeped in over the tops of his gum-boots as he knelt. He wished again that he had some company, even the horses: he felt young down there, and he remembered the feel of the house when he was small and had been left alone in it after dark.

He set his fuse and jog-trotted off to a safe retreat, padding between the tramlines, like the old horses, towards the light and the day that he could just see in the far, tiny distance.

Link stayed in the pasture with the horses, petting each one in turn, fondling them, talking, combing them, grooming their silly, fluffy little grey tails and telling tales to them about Ben Butch, and young Joe who had taken his job from him. Promising to come back to them later with some Archangel Tar for Thunder's back, he left them down by the stream and the alders. With his monkeyish shamble, he came to the crest, repeating to himself all that he had told the horses of his misfortunes. He saw the six full trams of coal standing harmlessly on the top and in a fit of delighted rage he ran down to them. He kicked out the sprags that held them safe and shoved the trams down the incline, into the mouth of the drift. He heard them roll, gather momentum, and finally crash, like the end of the world, somewhere down there. 'Who's top-dog, now, Ben Butch? Take you all day to clear that lot. Good old Tom; said I'd have my revenge, didn't I?'

CHAPTER 9

'It's no good you standing by that window, Floss, he hasn't had time to turn round yet. Why don't you go and lie down a minute? You want to be fresh for tonight.'

'Lie down? I got about fifty-nine jobs to do.'

'No, you haven't, you might as well relax for a bit, my girl; you've got the supper ready, I've seen it, and his clothes are all right, I been inspecting them. Think he'll wear that tie? It's on the quiet side for our Joe.'

'He's got to wear a respectable tie for chapel, he can say what he likes. Why did he have to promise to go up there today, knowing he was singing tonight? He makes me mad, that boy does. Stubborn! He's as bad as you.'

'He's doing a favour to them all, girl, they'll be able to get on with clearing and cutting now tomorrow. Piece-work, see, Floss; they want to fill the trams.'

'Well, I'd like to see him home, whatever. He's got to have food, have a bath, change, practise – I don't know.'

'There's no need to get mad now, Flossie; p'raps you should have called him earlier, but never mind, don't start worrying now.'

'That's right, blame me, as per usual. Nothing I do is right, is it? Ever?'

'Put a sock in it now, Floss, go and lie down a minute while I do my sniffs. You can't hope to see him for an hour or two, he can't rush a job like that.'

'Yes, a job like that, after all the school I gave him; sacrificing to send him to the Grammar and now he's no better than you. And what did he want to go to Ben Butch's for, when he had a tidy job with the Coal Board, I'd like to know?'

'I said enough when he started there, you were the one rolling his sleeves up for him then. Nobody listens to me in this house, of course. I've given up trying to talk.'

'Oh you.' Flossie wrinkled up her button nose at him, and retired exasperated to the scullery to make unnecessary custard. When she could find nothing else to do, she sat on the edge of a chair, as though waiting to spring, and looked vaguely at the television, the idleness of her hands grating on her like a rheumatic joint, like a stone in her shoe, her eyes moving again and again from the flick of the screen to the clock on the mantelpiece. She watched the clock, she stood at the window, then she walked to the garden gate to look up at the mountain. There was no sign of anyone; most of the fathers were in bed with the *News of the World* and the mothers were in chapel, comparing notes on the finery of the scrubbed, singing children.

Her mood changed from exasperation to a towering rage and she sat down again, flinging herself into a comfortable chair, and sulkily rehearsed her anger, and then suddenly, overwhelmingly, she was sick with anxiety. She went quite and still as fear took over. It was five o'clock. It was more than late.

Bryn was asleep with *Reynolds News* in front of the parlour fire. 'Bryn,' she said, 'Bryn, boy, he's still not back. Think we ought to do something?'

'What'd you say, what? W'as the time, then?'

'Bit gone five, and he's not back. Think you should go and look for him?'

'Jawch, it is a bit late, too, but you know how he is – hates a fuss. Look, gimme a cup of tea and pack some food and I'll go and meet him and he can eat a bit on the way down. P'raps he doesn't realise the time up there; time goes fast when you're busy and nobody with you. Aye, I'll do that and you go on to chapel and tell Fred he'll be a bit late, tell him to keep the solos to the end. One of us must go and tell Fred.'

They kept up their pretence of concern over the singing, she dared not release her fright into words. The surge of dread in the two of them was damped down, held, blanketed. To speak of it would acknowledge it, release it.

'Come on, then, get cracking, Flossie, and I'll go up. And you go on to chapel; we can't let old Fred down. Don't worry now, we'll manage fine, you just carry on.' She had handed him the reins, had retreated in womanish subservience, the spark of her under a vast bushel of unacknowledged, refused, rejected, commanding fear. She cut the food quickly, untidily, cutting too much, not knowing when to stop, what to decide, losing the knife and hunting for it in the litter on the table while she still held it in her hand. She dropped the loaf and as it rolled on the kitchen floor, she said, nerves on end, 'Oh, shut up,' to it.

'There you are, that's fine, Floss; that'll do grand. I'll go up in my good clothes and then I'll be ready to help him on, see. Come on, now, you change and off to go, to give Fred time to arrange the programme different. It'll be all right; I'll make sure he's clean, you watch.'

Flossie, numb and shocking in pink, went to the chapel, the biggest in the place, commandeered for the United Singing Festival – almost the only thing in which the chapels were ever united. Salem had been built in the grand Welsh-Gothic chapel-style at the turn of the century when God was real in the valleys in his white nightdress and flowing beard. She went to sit near the front to catch the eye of old Fred the Singing so that she could give her message without fuss, for fuss in chapel was a greater crime even than heresy, which was common enough among a people who felt on the whole that singing was more important than God or creed in the ordering of chapel affairs.

Fred was there, in excelsis, in the Big Seat – a tall, thin, pinched, draper of a man with a face like a horn-rimmed robin; beautiful, El Greco hands and the language of an infuriated long-distance lorry driver if the singing was flat and the deacons away. He wore his hair long and slack, and tossed it for rallentando and tore it for despair. He was dressed in black with a black bow-tie and a stand-up collar and carried for a baton one of his wife's steel knitting-pins stuck through with two corks. He noticed Flossie faintly mouthing at him and tiptoed down the aisle to her pew, looking like a nervous waiter. She covered her mouth with her pink gloved hand and whispered, 'I'm sorry, Fred, but Joe will be a bit late, he's been kept back doing a bit of over-time, so will you please put his pieces a bit later on in the programme?'

He was too full of his brief authority to notice the drawn and hunted look of her. 'Oh, damn me, Flossie, this is too bad. Damn it, I was relying on Joe. I wanted to start with something dramatic. I could hear the quiet in my mind, mun, with Joe singing "Comfort" to start. This has spoilt all my bloody plans, indeed it has.'

'Well, I'm sorry, Fred, I'm sure, but you'll have to alter it now. He's working late, and to tell the truth, he hadn't had his bath when I came out, but I came early to let you know, like.'

'It can't be bloody helped now. I'll have to go and rearrange things with Mock the Organ, then. All right, Flossie.'

She wriggled back into the corner of the hard shiny pew and fiddled with her gloves and then put on a brave show of indifference under her flowered hat and grey curls. She knew he couldn't have come yet and schooled herself not to look up at Bryn's seat in the gallery among the tenors. The chapel was filling up. The choir was almost complete. People filled the pew where she sat and then they brought benches out from the vestry and set them in the aisles for the overflow. In spite of herself, she looked up, but Bryn's place was still empty. If only they hadn't put those benches there she might have walked out; it was like being in jail, in that pew full of strangers. From where she sat, she could only see a few people that she knew: Sam and his wife from the Lion, Link among the bassers, Nell Link in a new puce hat that made her look like a piece of cheese, Joe Kremlin arguing about something, even in chapel – all of them looked unnatural and inhuman in their best and in her misery. No, Bryn wasn't there yet; give them time, Flossie girl, he's got to wash and change.

Cynthia had come to the service, in her brown suit and a little fur hat, with coral bright beads in a great chunk at her throat. She was excited and happy, watching for Joe, trying to see where he sat in the chapel, looking around with confidence and charm. There was a little smile in her face and the old fogies of colliers sitting near her wondered who she was and paid silent homage and envied some lucky devil.

In the back seat, nearest the door, Sal was sitting. She, too, was alone among strangers, but there was no assurance in her glance; she sat humble and shabby in pathetic finery, a big flat hat covering her dramatic hair and shadowing her big eyes. She had come half hoping to offer Joe an apology for her brother's behaviour, but was already reconciled to failure in that great crowd and in the press of an occasion.

Old Bryn, ill at ease in his best clothes, with fear churning up his bowels and tasting like blood in his mouth, job-trotted up the garden and on to the short-cut to the mountain. The setting sun was strong on his face and buzzed on his catarrh; there was a pain like a knife above his left eyebrow and down the side of his long nose. His left eye felt as though it were being pushed out of the socket. He was breathing short, through his mouth, and, as the climb steepened, panting like a dog, a tired old dog. He kept his eyes on the rounding path above him, kidding himself along that at any moment Joe would come springing down towards him, impatient and vital. He wished he had somebody with him, some company,

but Joe hated a fuss; no, he was better by himself. He wished
he had the breath to shout, to call Joe, but climbing in that red
sun it was hopeless.

He saw no one as he climbed, blind to the autumn, the
children's fire, the two grey horses that stood like carvings on
the crest of the pasture, aware only of his nose and his breath
and the horrible need to hurry. He put his rough left hand up
over his eye, pressed it down to the side of his nose and
shoved himself forward. The mountain was all still and silent.

There was no sign of his son at the workings, no sign of
life. His fear was now like some other creature that walked
beside him, or like some animal on his back. He stood helpless at the mouth of the drift, rigged out in his best, his
tenor's white shirt, his navy blue suit and his bowler hat.
'Joe,' he called into the tunnel, his voice ugly, like a caw. He
splashed a few yards down into the dark and then, suddenly
resolute, miner that he was almost from the cradle, he turned
back to the ramshackle office. The door was closed but not
locked, and he picked up a steel hat and a lamp and battery.
The hat was small on his big bumpy head, like a cockle-shell.
He saw Joe's old cap and hung his bowler beside it; near the
telephone were Joe's cigarettes and matches and when he
saw them he got a sudden unaccountable new lift of hope.
His cigarettes were there, the boy was all right. The weight
of the clumsy steel helmet pressing above his eyes helped the
pain there or at least changed the note of pain.

Bowed and stumbling, he sloshed in his best ginger shoes
down the silent incline. The beam of his lamp suddenly,
shockingly, caught the journey of trams, tossed, turned arse
over turned up tip, tangled, choking the drift, corking it up
tight. He tried to pull at them, he shouted, 'Joe, Joe, Joe boy,'
his breath wouldn't go further than his mouth, the dust was
killing him. He'd have to go for help, he was no bloody good
to man or beast. Oh, God, give me strength, if I can only shift
some of it. Then he remembered the telephone and fumbling,

stumbling, falling, battered by the irregularities in the roof, breathless, broken, he floundered into the daylight. He couldn't see to read the telephone book. 999 came from somewhere and when somebody answered his voice was a scream of impatient agony. 'For God's sake send somebody. My boy's in there, there's a journey on top of him. Get a doctor, and some colliers, strong ones, please, Miss. What? Where am I speaking from? From Ben Butch's, Brynhyfryd Colliery. Quick, for God's sake, quick.' He left the telephone dangling on its cord and ran again, stumbling, groping, back to the drift. Half-way down, he slipped on a slimy piece of rock, floured over with coal-dust, his struck the tram line and he was still unconscious when they came for Joe.

In her seat there by the door Sal was among the first to hear the hushed voices, awed voices that whispered, to see the cupped hands that hid mouths, the eyes that sharpened with horror and quickened with shock; something's happened to Joe Jenkins, accident. Bad? All up they say. She sat in her seat, pretending ignorance of Joe Jenkins, innocence of his hands, indifference to the crush of his mouth and his white thighs and flushed in a wave of panic that this might be her brothers' fault. She heard the whispers and the sigh that breathed over the congregation: something's happened to Joe, Joe, happened to Joe; she saw a sidesman walk with bent head and touch the shoulder of a little woman in pink and saw her move under a silly, silly hat. But the singing went on, Fred exhorted and pianissimo'd, but gradually the news spread to the gallery and the heart went out and the choir looked sick. Then Fred broke down, gave up his public, pulpit voice and said, 'All right, there's no shape to this. We all know why by now. We'll bring the meeting to a close with "Abide with Me" for Bryn and Flossie Jenkins.'

Cynthia was a stranger among them and nobody thought of telling her, she was still waiting and watching for Joe; she saw women openly crying and men unable to hold up their heads and was mystified. She turned to a woman beside her. 'What's the matter, why are people looking so upset?' she whispered. The woman's face crumpled, pitted, as she said, 'Young man been killed, boy from the village – oh, God, the price of coal.' Then Fred made his announcement and she understood. She couldn't face 'Abide with Me', couldn't face the chapel and the faces and the sorrow; she got up and left the place, hurried, hurried out, out to the air, out to the graveyard, and blundered on past the second tombstone on the right, oblivious of the grave of an earlier Joseph Jenkins.

She didn't think about how to behave; shocked and sick and obscurely excited, she ran away; the sentimentality of the role she was cast to play repelled her. She cried her rejection of the part at first more than the loss of Joe, she was suddenly angered by the drama and with what was foisted upon her. This melodrama had nothing to do with her or with Joe. She had to get away from it, out from the sentiment, out from the sick emotion. She ran out into the road and thumbed a lift and ran away and talked a little to the driver of the car about the weather.

Sall had always been religious in an inarticulate, Jesus-knows-all-about-my-troubles, feeble fashion and she found 'Abide with Me' very comforting. Its sickly sweetness pandered to her shallow emotions, gone thin and sugary with self-pitying self-indulgence. She had no right to cry for Joe, their intimacy gave her no rights, no privileges, but anybody could wipe away a tear under cover of a hymn, you didn't need rights for that much.

Wilf had been sent to bed, but the heat of the clothes made his burn hurt worse and he was standing in his grey shirt at the window, pressing his hand to the coolness of the glass and watching for the people to come out of chapel. He'd managed to hide his burn from his mother all day, but now, when he saw the size and glossy whiteness of his blister, he was weakening. He badly wanted comfort and sympathy, but he was realist enough, too, to remember that, though she'd soothe the burn and help that, she'd give him hell and tell his father. She'd sworn she'd tell his father the next time, and she never broke a promise, not of any kind. And Wilf knew his father.

Wilf's house was on the corner of Salvation Street and Repentance Street and from his window he could see the length of the main road and the turn down to Railway Street. The railway and the road and the river never parted company for long in Cilhendre and when he stood on tiptoes Wilf could see the lights on the river bridge and the bottom of the road that went to Ben Butch's mine. There was a street light opposite the chapel and he could see people beginning to come out; there was Joe's mother, running like the wind, and Jones the deacon chasing her, on a Sunday too. Then a girl came out and hitched a lift from a car and in a while the people all came out fast, belting out, not slow like chapel people, and all jabbering away, not talking respectable like Sunday. Wilf opened the casement window to listen to the conversations that passed under him. Two women under hats came by. 'The only child and all, God help poor Flossie.'

'And you hear them saying coal is too dear. They don't know the half of it.' Their voices went and a group of men came.

'Working overtime, was he?'

'Aye, Ben Butch had been without a fireman since Link chucked it and he asked Joe to blow a few holes today to let them get on tomorrow.'

'That's what comes of breaking the Sabbath.'

'Don't be so old-fashioned, William; think God did that to Joe or what?'

'Remember the Sabbath day and keep it holy.'

'We'll miss old Joe about the place, all right. Well, I'm going to the Club; I need a drink after a blow like that and Joe'd be the last to begrudge it. Anybody else coming?'

'For shame on you, I don't know what the world is coming to. I'm off home, whatever.'

'Be no harm in a drink, would there? We got to go down ourselves tomorrow.'

'Aye, come on; I'm not hanging about here – we can't do nothing – and if I go home now, I'll only sit and think. Come on, break this up.' The bowler hats moved away and now the people were passing in a rush, and Wilf saw Sam's father going down Railway Street, which wasn't his way home. Suddenly the people outside stopped hurrying and were standing still and looking over to the river bridge and the mountain. Nobody was speaking now, and Wilf climbed on to the chair by the window and he could see an ambulance crossing the bridge, and fussing, quick men jumped out and left the ambulance there. Accident; somebody's hurt; hope it isn't Joe that's had it, if Joe's going to hospital we won't have our money for the fireworks. Those men said something about Joe; oh, damn it all to hell, it is Joe, and now we won't be able to buy a rocket.

He climbed back into bed, slipped his bad hand under the smooth pillow and decided it would be all right to cry. It was cissie to cry because you wanted to tell your mother your hand was bad, but if you were mad and wanted to cry about the rocket it was all right.

CHAPTER 10

They didn't bring Joe home. The journey had caught him as he ran to safety before blowing the hole and the crash detonated the explosion so that the roof, the shot and the trams conspired together to mangle him, to crush and tear him. They didn't find all the pieces when eventually they got the way clear and the roof off, and they could only assemble the shape of a man on the stretcher and after the post mortem the coffin was kept in the mortuary until the last possible minute in case the mother should be tempted to remove the lid.

Flossie wanted Joe home. 'Bring me my boy, bring me my boy,' she shouted at them that first night, until the doctor gave her an injection and put her to sleep. But in the morning she had accepted defeat, had broken her heart and recovered her dignity. But a house of death was incongruous without a coffin; it was too empty, it posed new problems in the proper conducting of a funeral. When people came to offer sympathy the ritual demanded that they should be led into the parlour, to view the body and to pay their last respects; but here there was no body, nothing in the parlour, no pattern to follow, no way to behave. Flossie was doubly robbed.

She went passive and still and sat there in the kitchen in her incongruous, appropriate, black dress and the neighbours took her world into their hands. An almost continuous stream of sympathisers called, knocking at the front door, to indicate the formality of their visit. They had the ritual, the form, only Flossie and Bryn were without the props. They came in, subdued and slow, they murmured that they were sorry for their trouble and shook hands. They sat in the kitchen and said something nice about the boy and Flossie nodded and was far beyond speed or the reach of words. Her sole contribution was the formula, 'He was the apple of my eye.' She said it over and over and didn't know when she'd said it. And the sympathisers too had their formula. 'That's the price of coal, see, people don't know.'

Bryn couldn't indulge, drown in defeat, like Flossie; with Steve to support him, he had to attend the inquest, to make arrangements, to keep his head. His anger helped to sustain him, but his nerves were stretched to the limit of endurance. He broke on the Tuesday evening when, among those who came to pay their respects was a little widow, Jane Throw-Out, with her mentally defective son. His mother never went anywhere without the boy, in his slack waterproof and a navy-blue schoolboy's cap perched above his ever-young face. They went always arm-in-arm and he sat beside her, nodding and smiling in Flossie's kitchen. He was a co-operative young man, harmless and obedient and so eager to conciliate that all he ever said was, 'Oh, yes,' into any pause in conversation, or apropos of nothing. Compulsively, he said, 'Oh yes,' about once in every minute. His mother was sympathising with Flossie and Bryn, the price of coal had been mentioned and Flossie had said, 'He was the apple of my eye,' and the boy had said, 'Oh yes,' and 'Oh yes,' and 'Oh yes.' Suddenly, Bryn got up, his face working and the colour of yeast and, without a word to them, pushed past the visitors and out into the garden. Steve followed him out, making excuses, 'He's taking it bad, old Bryn, excuse me. I'll go and talk to him. 'Scuse me.'

Bryn was standing alone at the garden gate, his hands clenched over the top bar, and horrible, noisy, dry sobs were shaking his big, clumsy, collier's frame.

'Bryn, boy, Bryn.' Steve put out his hand, sensitive as a woman, on that big clutching right hand.

'Christ, Steve, I can't stand it. If any other bugger talks to me about the price of coal, I'll belt them a fourpenny one, indeed to God I will. The price of coal, the price of coal, can't they say anything else, can't they shut up? Can't they shut up?' His voice broke and his breath wouldn't come, past the sobs and the catarrh.

'Aye, I know, boy, I know. Take it easy now, take it easy.'

'Does she have to go on saying he was the apple of her eye? Tell her to stop it, Steve, tell her to stop it.'

'She can't, Bryn; leave her be, it's her safety-valve. It won't be long now, Bryn.'

'Won't be long? You don't know what you're talking about. It won't be long – it's for ever, you bloody fool.'

'I know, boy, I know. But the tension will pass, this sort of best-behaviour farce will pass.'

'Why don't they leave us in peace? I've heard the same things a hundred times today.'

'You wouldn't like it if nobody came; you always go yourself to sympathise, you never miss.'

'I'll miss after this, boy, all right.'

'Oh, Christ, Bryn, I'm sorry. I haven't got nothing else to say. Nobody has, we can't say nothing. Put up with us for a bit, Bryn, for Flossie's sake. All this is taking her mind a bit. Thank God you've got each other.'

'I'm not much to her, Steve, it was him she lived for. He was her life, see, not me. I don't know how things will be between us now – he was always a kind of insulation between her and me. We'll have to start fresh, with old tools. She's very far from me now; I don't think she realises that I've lost my boy too – her boy, not mine.'

'It'll work out, Bryn, she'll be needing all your strength.'

'There's no strength left in me. I can only offer the shelter of the stricken tree.'

'Better the stricken tree than no tree.'

'It was seeing that boy there finished me, see, that useless, helpless boy left and Joe gone. There's no sense in it, is there?'

'He's all his mother's got, too, she couldn't live without him. Are you coming back in?'

'No, not till she's gone. You come out and let me know when she goes. I couldn't stand "Oh yes," again tonight.'

'All right, then, stay you and I'll go back to Flossie.'

Link in the pigeon loft watched the two men and envied their friendship and felt horribly afraid. He clutched one of his warm, unwinking pigeons in his big hand, then he threw the bird up to join its fellows and, stooping, stepped out of the loft. He went through his own garden gate and crossed to Bryn when Steve had gone.

'Bryn, I'm very sorry for your trouble. There's no hard feelings, is there?'

'Thank you, Tom; no, no hard feelings.'

'He was a good boy, Bryn.'

'Aye.' They stood there in silence for a minute, nothing left to say. Bryn waited for it.

'That's the price of coal, see.' Bryn closed his eyes on his nerves and said, 'Aye. There it is, see. Started work again have you?'

'Aye, in Number 4. Well good night, then, Bryn.'

'Good night, Tom, and thank you.'

Steve left Bryn and Flossie to their separate agonies and went guiltily to the Lion, hoping that company and a drink or two would help to shift the look of the two of them from his eyes, the weight of their sorrow from his back, strengthen him to be strong for them again tomorrow. His guts tasted sour and his chest under the load of coal-dust was criss-crossed with steel bands, his face felt dry and tight with unshed tears and meaningless consolations. But the public bar was cold with shock, uncomfortable, guilty, unrelated. As Steve came wheezing in through the swing-door, his head on one side to see better with his good eye, his big nose pinched with misery, he knew he'd come to the wrong place, for the first words he heard, spoken into an earlier silence, like a sigh, were, 'Aye, there it is, see, such is life.'

'Give us a pint, will you, Sam?'

'Been down there with Bryn, Steve?'

'Just come from there.'

'How are they there?'

'Taking it bad, what the hell d'you expect?'

Steve picked up his pint and went to join the other drinkers around the stove. Krem and Dai Dialectic were there, with Fred the Singing and Sammy the Fish and Fruit.

'Terrible thing, Steve, isn't it, mun? Lovely voice the boy had, should have been trained, I always said. He could have been in the Carl Rosa easy.' Fred eased the spectacles on his robin's nose.

'What d'you think of the verdict, though, Steve? The bastards. There was no need to close the drift. That journey was sprigged proper on Saturday, wasn't it, Dai? We can swear to it, mun. There wasn't no negligence. It's just an excuse to get at Ben; the Coal Board don't like old Ben. Somebody shoved that journey down, as sure as my name's Jim.'

'Well the Enquiry said it was negligence, didn't they? They've taken Ben's licence from him, you can't do nothing about it now.' Sammy, as a business man, was a great supporter of the law.

'It's a bloody shame, that's what it is. All that coal lying there and us boys out of work now and ordering halves by here.'

'It's a fact, though, Steve; that journey was safe enough. Cross the Bible, it was. It never went down the incline by itself.'

'If it didn't go down by itself, somebody shoved it. All right. So what?'

'Well, good God, if somebody shoved it to kill Joe it's murder, mun, don't you realise?'

'Because somebody shoved it, it doesn't mean they did it to kill Joe; they could have shoved it to spite old Ben, not knowing Joe was down there at all.'

'Know what I've been thinking, quiet like? If it was murder, it's capital murder. The bloke would get hung.'

'Why, for God's sake?'

'Well you know this new law, you can still get hanged if you kill somebody by making an explosion. I know that because I was interested in the explosion part.'

'Who you going to blow up then, Krem? The House of Lords?'

'No, fair play now, listen. That journey hit Joe when he was going to blow up that hole, right? The impact made the thing go off too soon, so Joe gets the firing as well as the journey on top of him. It's like a cannon in billiards, see, the bloke with the cue made the cannon, didn't he? All right; the bloke shoved that journey made the explosion, and he killed a man by making an explosion, right? O.K. Capital murder. He could swing for it.'

'No, Krem, you're wrong; even if somebody did help that journey down, it was accidental death all the same. Who was to know Joe was there, and who was to know Joe would be firing just then? Too bloody far fetched, mun.'

'Don't start saying things like that about the place, Krem, there's a good boy; things is bad enough as they are. Let Bryn and Flossie think it was a pure accident, whatever. Give them that much. Let it lie, boy.' Steve's voice was tired, depressed beyond belief.

'Nobody will ever convince me that journey took off by itself, Steve.'

'Nor me, neither. Jim and me saw those sprags Saturday, Official Enquiry or not. There wasn't no negligence and Ben shouldn't have lost his licence. Good God, ask old Cyril Toupee, if you don't believe us. He's such a bloody old woman, he fussed about that journey Saturday like a hen with chicks; didn't he, Jim?'

'Aye, I still maintain somebody shoved it. What about them blokes Joe had a fight with, Dai? Told us all about it, didn't he?'

'Too true, he did. Sall Ever Open Door's brother and a couple of young fellers knocked him out and warned him to keep off Sall – or else.'

'I never heard it.'

'You don't know everything, Sammy Fish, you and all your old women in that bus of yours. You knew, didn't you, Steve?'

'I knew he'd been in a fight, that's all.'

'And then, there were those Germans as well,' Jim was warming up again, 'one of them was after Joe's girl, I heard. You never know with them old Nazis. Look what they did to the Jews, for a start. And all the Russian women they raped.'

'Oh, Jim, chuck it, will you? Those German boys were mostly kids in the war. They might as well say you were an imperialist aggressor.'

'Who, me? Me an imperialist? Have you gone mad or something, Steve Williams?'

'The same thing applies, doesn't it? You're British, aren't you?'

Fred the Singing put his beak into the discussion. 'If somebody did shove that journey, I'd say it was to spite Ben, though; wouldn't you?'

'Well, we all know who'd cut Ben's throat tomorrow, don't we? No names, no pack drill.'

'Who d'you mean? Link?'

'No names, boyo, no names.'

'Aye; come to think, Mrs Link was crossing swords with Flossie no later than last week outside my bus.'

'He'd do it, too, would Link. Look at him, mun, I can just see him, can't you, kicking the sprags out to make work for Ben clearing it all out.'

'No, Krem, no. There's no harm in old Link. Nobody can help the way he looks, for God's sake. Look at us five for a start – there's a gallery of oil-paintings to come home to.'

'Well, my money's on Link. Ten to one the field. Any takers?'

'Hell of a time to try and make a joke, Krem.'

'Aye, indeed; sorry I'm sure. No offence.'

They turned to their beers.

'You'll be pegging this week, then?'

'Aye, not for long, I hope, the dole don't go nowhere, mun, won't cover the never-never for a start. If they take the telly back the missus will break her heart and turn to Bingo.'

Steve pushed his half-empty glass to one side. 'I think I'll go home, boys, there's no heart in me tonight. Don't go on about that capital murder thing, Jim bach, you know what this village is; the women would crucify Link with their tongues, and his wife is a decent enough sort. Don't start anything.'

'But, Steve, wait a minute. If that bugger did kill Joe, wouldn't you like to see him swing for it?'

Steve got up slowly, his breath tight but the anger sharp in his good eye. 'No, Jim Kremlin, I wouldn't want anybody to swing – not ever, not for anything. I like to think I'm a civilised man, not a barbarian. Your friend Mr Stalin was a great believer in liquidating chaps. A great old executioner he was. I'm not, thank you. Good night, now, and don't forget now, Krem: shut your bloody mouth.'

'O.K., Steve, O.K. Good night, then.'

They watched him go and heard his terrible cough as the cold, fresh air hit him in the doorway. 'The coal's got old Steve right enough, but he can say what he likes, there's some deserves liquidation. We don't know all the sides of the question, see, do we? You watch. Stalin will come to his own yet, wait you. Where would they have been without him in Russia, I ask you?'

Knowing Ben Butch as they did in Cilhendre, no one was satisfied with the verdict that Joe's death had been due to Ben's
negligence. They knew perfectly well that Ben would not
have risked losing a whole journey; Ben wanted that coal,
he'd have seen that the journey was properly sprigged. If it
wasn't negligence, then it was malice, it was spite – spite
against Ben or young Joe. And the wicked, unanswered question 'Who?' hung about the village, lowering, like the smell
of burnt rubber. Jim Kremlin dropped his theory of capital
murder since his promise to Steve, but Sammy the Fish whispered it over the potatoes and pears as his cold hands weighed
up pieces of hake and the shopping women bought it with the
carrots and onions. No names were mentioned, no pack drill,
but theories and speculations bounced like rubber balls across
the garden fences and over the clothes lines. A man over a
pint caught another's eye with a suggestion, a husband speculated to his wife in the bed-time quiet and the wives behind
the shelves at the Self-Service whispered and hinted and
always added, 'But don't let on I said anything, mind.'

Mrs Link heard the rumours and leapt to her husband's
defence. She stood on the pavement when the women were
gathering around Sammy the Fruit and Fish and swore that
her Tom had been in the singing in the morning and had spent
the afternoon in bed. Fat, slack and cheese-coloured, she
waved a parsnip in her hand and shouted defiance, like
Boadicea, and threatened everyone who slandered her
husband with a solicitor's letter. Then the tears began to run
down her flabby cheeks and she couldn't wipe them away
because her hands were full of vegetables. The neighbours
immediately abandoned Sammy, and put their arms around
Nell and took her into one of the houses and made a cup of
tea for her, while she put down her burden and wiped her
face with her canvas apron.

'Nobody's accusing your Tom, Nell fach, no, indeed to
God; it's those Germans, if it's anybody, I've said all the

time. But the Enquiry said it was accidental death and they ought to know, for goodness' sake.'

'Yes, indeed, Nell, don't carry on. Take no notice, they'll have somebody else to pull to pieces in a day or two. Don't let on you care, don't give them the satisfaction.'

'Here you are, Nell, nice cup of tea, look. Nothing like it, is there? Don't cry now. Got the depression, is it? Your age, see, comes to us all. This will blow over again.'

'But why should they pick on my Tom? He wouldn't harm a fly; look how he loves them old pigeons and everything.'

'Yes, of course, Nell; old gossip it is, don't worry. Like I say, it'll all pass, you watch. How is Tom taking it himself, then?'

'He hasn't said a word out of his mouth to me about it. But I know he's upset in himself, off his food and all.'

'Poor fellow, too. Not nice, is it, taking a man's character for nothing like that? And the man in bed all the time, if you please.'

CHAPTER 11

Mrs Griffiths and Cynthia were in the living-room behind the shop. Mrs Griffiths, behind a pair of formidable spectacles, was sitting at the table surrounded by account books, while Cynthia sat in an armchair beside the fire. She held a poker in her hand, with which she teased and fiddled with the fire. There was a sulky, wilful expression on her face.

'I don't care what you say, Mam, I'm not going there; that's final.'

Mrs Griffiths drew one of her deep sighs. 'But it looks so bad, Cyn, it's rude. I feel awful about it.'

'Look, if I'd been engaged to Joe, or if I'd ever met them, I'd go; but I'm not anything to them. They've never even seen me. I'd have to say who I was and everything. And if I went, what could I do, what could I even say?'

'Well, I'd come with you. I could talk to them. If only you'd go, to show you know the way to behave, for goodness' sake.'

'I'm to go as a screaming sacrifice to your ideas of what's proper, am I? No, don't keep on, Mam, please. I've said no and I mean no. I don't want to go.'

'I don't understand you, I don't indeed. You're so hard, girl, I don't know what's come over you.' She didn't answer and the silence lengthened between them. Mrs Griffiths wrote out several times, 'A settlement would oblige' and wrote a cheque to the wholesalers. Cynthia fiddled with the poker and sat bent over the fire, huddled up, withdrawn.

'Make a cup of tea, then, will you, Cyn? I'm a bit tired with all these old 'counts.'

Cynthia got up slowly from her chair, moving as if she were sick, holding herself as though she were afraid that her stomach was about to fall out. She filled a kettle and put it on the stove, standing over it, with her hand on the shiny handle, her eyes glazed over and staring. Her mother's exaggerated show of grief and shock had sickened her; she hated its hollowness, its conventionality, its prescribed form, its pat- terned, proper responses. Her mother's friends and customers offered her their sympathy, but to Cynthia it seemed only their habitual interference and compulsive concern with other people's lives. She felt dirtied by their condolences, dimin- ished by their fellow-feeling; their intrusions weakened, broke down, the slim defences she had put up to preserve her pride from them. There were moments when the memory of Joe's laugh or his kisses or his jealousy swept over her like a blush, but she set herself to refuse them, to reject them, least anyone should begin to regard her as an object of pity. No one was to be allowed to pity her, no one. Her mother's friends shook their heads over her and gave each other understanding glances of superior knowledge and toleration, for which she could have killed them. She jerked herself from the stove and turned on her mother with a sudden furious dart:

'–Drawing the curtains and trying to make me wear black, like a Victorian Miss. My life is not blighted, my heart isn't broken for ever. I'm sorry, I can't play up. He's dead. O.K. I'm sorry, terribly sorry. I'll miss him. I do miss him and I'm terribly sorry for his mother – Flossie, he called her' – her voice weakened, wavered for a moment, and then rose to a small desperate shout – 'but I'm alive, Mam, I'm going on, see.' There was a ragged fringe to her voice as she went on, 'Now shut up about it, shut up, shut up. Finish. I'm not going there and I want you to leave me alone. Understand? Leave me quite alone.'

'All right, love, I won't say another word. I'm sorry, I'm sure. Sit down now, I'll make the tea.'

'Don't start treating me like an invalid, either. I tell you I'm all right.'

'Yes, love. You make it, then. Oh, there's the shop. I'll just see who it is, the tea'll have made by the time I get rid of them.'

'Don't you talk about me. Don't you dare.'

'No, Cyn, I won't, come you.'

Lil Cream Slices was in the shop with her friend, Mrs Morgans Don't Care. 'Hullo, Mrs Griffiths, how's young Cyn now? Broken down, has she? – nothing like a good cry, is there, fair play.'

'Cyn's all right, thanks Lil. No, she hasn't broken down, she knows best how she feels. It's not for us to say. Can't bear to go there, you know how it is, but I'll send a little wreath from the two of us; looks better, don't you think?'

'Yes, that'll be lovely, Mrs Griffiths. What'll you send? Chrysanths and maidenhair is very nice this time of the year. Always likes a bit of maidenhair myself.'

'I'll have to see what they've got down in Swansea. There's still plenty of choice about. Did you want anything from the shop, Lil?'

'No, I only came in to ask how she was, like.'

Cynthia heard Lil's voice from the sitting-room, and, determined as she was to preserve her integrity or whatever it was she was guarding, she came like a little toreador into the shop. 'Hullo, Lil, hullo, Mrs Morgans. Filthy night, isn't it?'

'Awful, girl; I just popped in to see if your mother'd got those stretch stockings in yet – my legs is so fat gone, if I don't get the stretch, I can't get them high enough to cover my knees and reach my knickers.'

'No, like I was saying, Lil, they haven't come in yet, but they should be here before Sunday for you.'

'That's all right, then.'

Cynthia stood her ground. 'Mam, that tea I made for you will be black if you don't come.'

'Oh, sorry to keep you back, Mrs Griffiths fach, I'm sure. We'll be off, won't we, Mrs Morgans? Good night, then, both. Good night now.'

'So long, then, so long.'

'No need to be so short with them, Cynthia, they mean well, you know that.'

'O.K., they mean well, O.K.; but they can mind their own affairs as far as I'm concerned. I won't let them. Close the shop now, will you? I'll lock the front door and you put the light out, then we won't have any more kind sympathisers, will we?'

'Oh dear, dear,' her mother breathed. 'Oh dear, dear.'

CHAPTER 12

Wilf's burn was festering and Sam was worrying about it.

'Look, Wilf, I know what we'll do. You come home with me after school dinner and we'll tell my father about it, is it?'

'But he'll tell my father.' Wilf looked shrunken, smaller than ever.

'No, we'll make him promise, and then he won't. He'll put ointment on it and a pink plaster and make it better, is it? Come on, mun, Wilf, there's no good just standing crying by that wall. We got to do something.'

'Are you sure he won't tell?'

'Of course he won't if he's promised, don't be daft.'

'All right then if you're sure, sure as spit in your eye.'

Steve was sworn to secrecy on his Bible oath, made to spit on one finger, then wipe it and say,

'See this wet, see this dry,
Kill my mother if I lie.'

He shook his head and whistled when Wilf slowly, but trustingly, held out his little, fat, grubby hand, with the flesh raw and yellow across the palm.

'Got a burn there all right, Wilf. And you didn't tell anybody? Well, well, you're very brave, no doubt, but you shouldn't play with fire, boy bach, no indeed. You've had your lesson all right, haven't you, eh?'

'Yes. It's hurting.'

'No doubt it is. Wait you now. We'll have to clean it first. Steve will make it better in a minute. Leave it to old Steve, isn't it?'

'Yes.'

'Drop of warm water and disinfectant, and a bit of cotton-wool. There we are; stings a bit, I know, but we got to clean it, see, love. There, there's a brave boy, isn't he, Sam?'

'Aye. 'Course he is.'

'Where did you get this burn then, Wilf?'

'Sunday it was. We was up the mountain playing before the singing, and we was playing gorillas and they went a bit rough so I lit a fire instead.'

'Playing gorillas is it? Funny sort of game. Don't think I used to play gorillas in my young day. Lions and tigers more.'

'Well, we was playing gorillas 'cos we saw Link, and Geraint said we was his relatives, isn't it, Sam?'

'Aye, that's right enough. And then Wilf lit this fire and got his burn and we put the fire out. Peed on it we did, Dad, and then Joe came and said we was late and we'd cop it if we didn't go home quick.'

'Oh, aye. Poor Joe. You were talking to him, were you?'

'Yes, going to work he was. Are you going to his funeral?'

'Yes, I'm going. Is your father?'

'Yes. My mother was brushing his bowler hat. We won't be able to buy a rocket now, 'cos Joe didn't finish giving us the money for it. It's a pity Joe died, isn't it? Joe was nice to us, wasn't he Sam?'

'Aye, old Joe was all right, he was.'

'See anybody else up the mountain then?'

'No, nobody else, did we, Wilf?'

'No, only Link going to see his relatives and then Joe and then we went to the singing. Is it going to get better?'

'Yes, it'll be all right, Wilf. We'll put a plaster on, like this, see, so the air can get in, and you come tomorrow again, for me to put more of this powder on it. This is very special powder, best thing for burns. But don't light no more fires, good boy, will you? And we'll keep it quiet, right?'

'Right. Thank you very much, Mr Williams.'

'That's all right, Wilf. And here's thrippence to put in with your money for the fireworks. Keep it safe now.'

'Oh, thank you.'

'Thanks, Dad mun. How much we got now, Wilf?'

'Here it is, you count. Sam's a better scholar than me, Mr Williams.'

'Better for sums, p'raps. I expect you're better for other things.'

'I'm the best to light fires, and I'm the best Jap, 'cos I'm the smallest.'

'We got three and a penny, now. Not all from Joe, see, we been saving ourselves as well. Let's go and tell the others we got this thrippence, Wilf. You never know, we may get that rocket yet. So long, Dad.'

'Hey, half a minute, boys. You don't want me talking about that burn, right?'

'Oh no, Mr Williams, please.'

'All right, then. We'll make a bargain. I won't say about that burn, if you don't say about Link going up the mountain that morning. There's no need to go saying about the place that you saw him. It's none of our business, is it? He was p'raps doing something private, and none of us likes having our private affairs talked about all over the place. You know what the women in Cilhendre are. You don't want them all getting at you, do you, Wilf? So you keep Link's business quiet too.'

'O.K., Dad; no, we won't say, will we, Wilf?'

'No.'

'So long, then.' Steve watched as Wilf restored the match-box to his pocket with his good hand and then gently tucked his clean, sore hand into his other pocket with infinite care. Then Sam charged away, shouting, 'Race you to the top of the road, Wilf, come on.'

Steve threw away the warm water and tidied up his first-aid box. Link had gone up the mountain just before Joe on Sunday, then; but his wife swore he was in bed. He must have gone up straight after the singing in the morning to have

got there before Joe. Bryn said Joe only stopped for a mouth-
ful of food. But Link wasn't to know Joe was going into the
drift. And he only had the children's word for it, after all. But
they had no reason to lie about that. God knows they were
terrible fibbers when it suited their book, but why should
they have made up a story like that? No, that playing gorillas
seemed to clinch it. But if Link had been up the mountain it
didn't mean he'd sent the journey down. It could be a coincidence; but Steve felt it wasn't a coincidence. He hated
himself for thinking like this about Link. He hated the fact of
suspicion and the way the suspicion would inevitably warp
his relationship with Link; the falseness, the dishonesty that
would always be between them now. There hadn't hitherto
been any close relationship between them; they were neighbours, drank together, voted the same way, went to the same
chapel; but now there existed a kind of bond between them,
Steve would have to think about Link when he talked to him,
watch what he said to him, watch himself, watch him. Steve
hated that, hated himself for giving time to this corrosive suspicion, but the suspicion came without his bidding. Out of
work, as he was, he spent time thinking about people, knew
almost everything that went on in the village and gathered
news and impressions and nuances on his Death Club visits.
Thrown out of the working life of the place, he clung, like
one in fear of drowning, to its social and emotional life. But
it was time he changed his clothes for the funeral; time he
went to help Bryn and Flossie over their last formal hurdle
before they were left alone to live their loss.

The Nazi bombs had taken the roof off Swansea Market and
let the sun in. On the day of Joe's funeral the sun beat a tom-
tom on the colours and the smells there. Beat on the bronze
and clean-cut yellows of chrysanthemums, on bright green
sprouts and cauliflowers, on the polished, cold-green apples
and the warm-brown potatoes and Conference pears; on the

Welsh-wool blankets, honeycombed with colour; on the cruel red of meat and the nasty green of artificial parsley. Beat on the green painted stalls and underlined the white Welsh names: Tudor Griffiths, Welsh Wool; Thomas the Meat, hard to beat; Elias Davies, Carmarthen Butter, Try our Cheese. The sun drew out the smells: the sea-smell of laver-bread and cockles, the heavy, sick smell of meat, the old, old smells of second-hand books, the exciting smell of mouth-watering faggots and peas.

Sall walked through the colours and the smells and the noise and the selling. She wanted laver-bread and cockles for her brothers. In her shabby grey coat, with her basket and her plastic bag, she was humble and poor, pale with her big, beggar's eyes. They didn't bother to solicit her at the flower stalls; no one said, 'Lovely chrysies, love, only sixpence each.' She walked in the sun to the far corner where the second-hand books were and bought three battered murders for a shilling. She passed the plump, plucked chickens, the yellow farm butter, the Caerphilly cheeses fat as butchers, the Toys and Jokes stalls where the children were buying jumping jacks and sparklers and boxes of caps for cowboy guns; passed the wool stalls where striped flannel shirts and grey flannel colliers' drawers looked like indecent flags in the daylight and turned her eyes away from the nursing shawls to womb Welsh babies, like tents.

The clink of the cockle-shells in her basket irritated her and she stopped to make a platform of books on the top of them and set the squishy cow-pat laverbread on top of the books. As she knelt to sort her basket she saw a bucket standing at a flower stall. There were pink roses in the bucket, big pink rosebuds. A cynical florist had scattered water over the buds and drops were still held in some of the tips. She thought of Joe as she saw them, remembered him, missed him again, but she didn't know why the roses made her think of Joe, of love. She went up to the stall-holder.

'How much are the roses, please?'

'Bit dear, love, last of the season, see. Shilling each. Let you have the dozen for eleven bob.'

'Oh, they are dear, aren't they?'

'Look, tell you what I'll do, give you the dozen for ten shillings. Robbing myself, mind, but I can see you fancy them.' The woman whipped a dozen out of the bucket, shook off the water and wrapped them up in a white poke of tissue paper. 'Look, lovely, aren't they? Ten bob, is it?'

Sall paid over the note and took them from her. She looked down on them in the crook of her arm and smiled. As she walked on through the market the roses gave her confidence and she spent the last of her money on some grapes for her mother.

She went out into the burst and bombarding of the traffic in Oxford Street and with the reality of the traffic came the realisation of what she had done. Spent ten shillings on flowers. What on earth had come over her? The smell of the roses came up to her. Never mind, she thought, they'll be nice for Mam in the bedroom.

As she waited in the bus queue at St Mary's Church she was ashamed of the flowers. What would people think? She tried to put on a bold face, to pretend she was the sort of person who bought flowers; she looked around at the people passing her, at the restored church, at the big pub on the corner, and she held the flowers downwards, hidden in their paper wrapping. She felt the wet paper through the cotton gloves, felt the incongruity of them, felt they were strident, like the gargoyle over the pub across the way, which people said was meant to be Satan making faces at St Mary's. She no longer thought about Joe; she'd forgotten the odd unrecognised trick her memory had played on her when she first saw the roses. She believed she'd bought the roses as flowers for the dead; a wreath, a 'floral tribute'.

She found a seat at the far end of the red bus and as it lumbered up the valley, rocked with gossip and greeting, she tried to imagine what her brothers would say about the flowers. They'd guess she'd bought them because of the funeral, they'd know. As the now almost empty bus drew near her stop, she looked around to see that no one was looking and then pushed the flowers under her seat and left them. She'd say she'd lost a ten-shilling note somewhere.

Number 4 Colliery epitomised for many old colliers all that had gone awry with their dreams of public ownership. In the highly mechanised, last-word efficiency of Number 4, nationalisation was felt to be almost synonymous with mechanisation and the skilled, proud craftsmen of colliers felt demoted, like bits of wheels, lengths of chain; men had become man-hours, work was measured in feet and inches instead of tons and tramloads. After the slap-dash, slap-happy, personal responsibility of Ben Butch's small mine, Link felt insecure and insignificant in Number 4. The infernal noise of the mechanical coal-cutters and the conveyor belts shattered on his nerves, already raw with guilt and fear. Strange faces looked at his ugliness afresh, strange colliers, whose reliability he hadn't proved with the years, worked on either side of him and made him fearful of the roof, and he missed the civilising, humanising influence of men's pride in their own stalls, and faith in the roof they maintained themselves. And, worst of all, the conveyor belt wasn't like a horse; was no company, was no one to talk to.

He went out of work early for Joe's funeral; went with many others who had played football against Joe, who had sung in pubs and chapels with him, who had drunk pint for pint with him, who remembered him. Link stood in the cage with some of them in the belly-dropping ascent to the top; they talked about Joe there and went on talking through the steam of the shower baths and in the sudden hospital quiet of the lamp-room. That was when Link first realised that Joe's regular girlfriend worked in the office at Number 4. He heard the men praise her, call her a game little thing, say she had a word for everyone and was as pretty as sin, and he felt an overwhelming compulsion to see her, to know what she looked like, to think about her with Joe, picture her. He could think of no excuse then that would take him to the office, but he'd go, he'd go soon, somehow. He'd find an excuse before long.

He was silent, brooding, ugly among the strangers at the bus-stop, fear always low in his belly, like a lump of grey porridge. He stood behind the others at the stop, his tweed cap pulled low and straight over his brow, the washed-out khaki scarf at his throat intensifying his drab, collier's pallor, his shadowed eyes watching, suspicious, stupid.

The undertaker deputed Link, since he was one of the neighbours, to help carry out Joe's coffin, and Steve Williams watched his face as he took the weight on his shoulders, but there was nothing in his face, no sorrow, no sympathy, no shame, no fear, nothing – as though ugliness left no room. Steve had expected to feel murderous towards Link in that defeated house, but the thought that came was, 'Christ, what the poor devil must be feeling, if it's true! God help him.'

CHAPTER 13

Over the door of the canteen in Number 4 was printed the warning, 'Spitting and Smoking Strictly Forbidden'. It was more than a mere warning about smoking and spitting, it was a warning of what was in store, a threat of the cleanliness therein, of the scrubbed, mind-your-manners, tea-in-the-parlour atmosphere. On the whole, the colliers avoided the canteen, preferring to eat in the warm, black, known, familiar coal-face, the sandwiches and biscuits going black-finger-marked to their coal-caked lips and the tea stone cold in their bottles. But when a man had a bus to wait for and a long journey to his own valley, the canteen was a stop-gap waiting-room, a cold-comfort shelter.

Cynthia was taking her afternoon cup of tea there; she sat alone at a table on the far side, the executive, clean-clothes, top side of the canteen, and talked across the room to the colliers on the other side, the door side, the coal-face side, the humble side, where the colliers slid into the canteen and sat, quickly, near the door, humble still, apologetic, in a hang-over, left-over attitude of apology for their unsociable dirt – an attitude that hung on in spite of pit-head baths and the change of clothing in their lockers. They sat in their tweed caps, check shirts, mufflers and shabby tweed jackets, wind-breakers, cast-off uniforms, service blouses, their eyes still rimmed with coal, like those of sultry beauties, and their eye-lashes long and seductive because of the vaseline they used at home to get the coal off.

They bantered with Cynthia, flirted with her, appreciated her, respected her. The word had gone around that she wanted no sympathy, that her young man's name was taboo;

this they understood and approved, it saved embarrassment, she was wise, right.

Link sat on the fringe. He too sat alone at a table, silent, ugly, pallid, tense, watching her under the shadow of his peaked cap. He knew now that this was Joe's girl, this beauty, this wet-dream perfection, this girl. And he had taken her away from Joe, had robbed Joe of her, had been able to deny her to Joe. He felt he had a right now to her; he had taken her from him, she was in a sense now his, his own, by right of conquest. Those others sitting there talking so free to her, they didn't know. They didn't know that he and she had a special relationship; they talked, but he was nearer to her; they had no rights, no business. He watched her. She picked up the big, coarse, NCB-stamped mug, like a boulder in her delicate hands; when she lifted it to her mouth it almost covered her face, she peeped over the top of it like a baby. He watched the yellow beads at her throat, saw them move with her breathing, and he watched them slip sideways to encircle her breast as she bent over to pick up her bag from the floor. He watched as she turned in her chair to drape her jacket over her shoulders. Then she pushed the chair back and stood and was small and neat, and her legs–. She had a way of throwing back her head as she walked, tossing her hair, and she was straight and small. She called good-bye to the men and came up to the door. He stood and went to the door and opened it for her. She smiled, said thanks, without seeing him, and went through. He followed her outside and she stood under the No Smoking, No Spitting sign and felt in her bag for a cigarette. He was behind her, and her hair was brown and crisp and his breath moved it.

'Would you like a cigarette?' he said, his voice hoarse, male, rough.

'Oh, I didn't know you were there. You gave me a start. Well, thank you very much, I was just looking for one. Thanks.' He held a match and watched as her cheeks pulled in with the pull of the air and she let the grey smoke out and said 'Thanks' again and the smoke came in little wisps between her teeth.

'I'm from Cilhendre, like,' he said, the 'like' saying everything, all that she refused to hear. Her face went cold, haughty, with the pride in her that would let no one think of her, expose her, denude her, turn her over like second-hand clothes, like something in a jumble sale. Her grief was private, inviolate, her arrogance demanded, insisted upon this respect, this honour, this silence. She looked at Link, at his ugliness, his odious hideousness, and her face changed again. Pity and shame weakened her; she could not be firm and strong before this pathetic, humble, fumbling, ugly man.

'You're new here, are you?'

'Yes. I live near Joe's father.'

'Oh, yes.' The name, he'd actually said the name, by name. Why didn't he go away? Link couldn't let her go. He had to hold her there, keep her somehow, in the cold wind on the top of the pit. It was very cold after the canteen. The wind came across the top from the Brecon Beacons, November cold and bleak, tearing around the red-brick engine houses, flicking coal-dust off the tips like black sand, howling in the winding gear, tossing the streamers of steam that leaked like ectoplasm from the endless, rusty pipes overhead and rattling the grey, neatly forbidding wooden office building where soon she would go and be lost to him. She began to move away, across the packed coal-dust which was the earth, pock-marked with black rain puddles, each with its diminutive waves and tides in that high wind; she crossed the railway lines, delicate like a kitten, and passed beside the trucks piled with coal. He followed her. Soon she would reach the parked management cars outside the office. He must say something.

'My name is Tom. Tom Davies.'

'Oh, yes.' She smiled again, but didn't stop. He walked with her. He had to keep her.

'Well, back to work again, Mr Davies; it's very cold after the canteen, isn't it?' Her hand was on the knob of the door. 'I'll see you about. I'm sure. So long now, then.'

She'd gone. She closed the door on him and he stood and looked at the grey paint of the door and the brass knob she had turned. She closed the door on him and stood for a moment before it, her back to the room, to the others. The door between them; the door shut now on his face, on his threat to her determination, her resolve. She shut the door on him and shut up her mind, closed it to the seduction, the weakness, the pry of sympathy. This she could do in public, in the face, the stimulus of danger, her pride in control; but in her dreams she was nightly shattered, seduced, raped; night after night she saw him and always coming towards her, with a smile and his arms reaching. But she turned to the room, her head thrown back; her face, her pride her own.

He left the door and shambled to the bus-stop, a smile in his mind, a triumph; impervious to the cold, warmed by his possession, her acknowledgement, his right, his claim.

CHAPTER 14

In the pub and over the garden fences at the fruit cart and in the Co-op, in the works buses and in the colliers' train, the people of Railway Street debated the problem of Guy Fawkes' Day; should they this year have their usual celebration? In the end it was decided that Joe would have preferred it, that he would have hated to disappoint the kids, that life went on regardless.

Jim Kremlin and Dai Dialectic had not yet started work, and they appointed themselves, with Steve Williams, as official collectors for the Bonfire. Krem and Dai did the active jobs and Steve did the organising. They combed the mountains for kindling, begged every box from the Co-op, stole boxes from Sammy the Fish, who was a business man and therefore reluctant to give, denuded the paper-shop of back numbers and picketed the chip-shop in case anyone should take papers there on a barter system; and they organised a campaign for the use of toilet paper, since newsprint was at a premium. They levied a firework charge of half a crown on every household in the street and threatened Sammy the Fish with a boycott if he didn't sell them a bag of potatoes at cost price. Then they divided the potatoes out among the housewives to share out the task of making chips for the Guy Fawkes' party. Mrs Jones From the Country made small beer and elderberry wine and she was excused chip duty in return for several of her bottles. At the Lion they collected from the drinkers and made a secret cache of beer bottles, strictly for Gentlemen only. Jenkins the Oil gave them two gallons of paraffin instead of the half-crown firework money and the Italian promised the fireworks cheap if they bought them all from him.

But there was always the problem of the chair for the top of the fire, the chair for the guy to sit enthroned before his destruction. The chair was a recurrent problem, for who would want to give away a chair, after all? They tried the minister, but there were no old chairs in the chapel; they tried Sam the Lion, but he had nothing shabby enough to give away; the grocer's widow refused to answer the door to them and the problem of the chair remained. Meanwhile, they made the guy. Old clothes were particularly hard to find since the colliers all wore their old clothes to rags underground and a female guy wouldn't do at all. Finally, they spotted Jim Whitmarsh's scarecrow. Jim Whitmarsh, the Man Who Won the War, lived in Runaway Terrace, so Railway Street owed him no loyalty; he was a market gardener in a small way and one of the few people in Cilhendre who had been called up. He'd never seen action except in the Pay Corps, but had earned two proud stripes and never let his glory fade. Indeed, so firmly were those stripes established in the village that streaky bacon was always called Jim Whitmarsh in the Co-op. Since summer was well and truly finished, Krem and Dai felt no real compunction in strip-teasing the scarecrow after dark one night and leaving a notice pinned to its nudity which said, 'Thanks, Corp.'

They were beginning to despair over the chair when Krem thought of woodworm. 'Dai, boy,' he said, 'I got it. Woodworm.'

'Jim bach, you can't have woodworm, not without you got a wooden leg on the sly.'

'No, mun, it's the answer. We got woodworm in the house. They're in that old furniture the missus had after her mother. I been shouting about it for years, and they're just the job for the fire; full of it, stinking with it they are. Wait you, we'll go home now. We'll manage, you watch. Now here's the gen.'

*

Mrs Krem looked very suspicious when they turned up in the private middle of her morning, placatory and ingratiating. 'What's the game, boys, what you two plottin' by there?'

'Plottin'? What the hell you talking about, Bron? Can't I have a bit of a rest in my own house, that's nearly paid for, after all the collecting and stealing we've been doing. Sit down, Dai mun, take the weight off your feet for a bit. Got a cup of tea there, Bron?'

'Cigarette, Bron?'

'Thanks, Dai. Got everything, then?'

'Pretty well, girl, pretty well. Still short of the chair, that's all. Got any ideas yourself?'

'Who, me? No, not I; who'd be so daft to give you a chair, good boy, to burn?'

'We got to have a chair, see. Damn, I wish I could think of something, honest.'

'I see your friends have let off another bomb yesterday.'

'Don't you start on politics now, our Bron, you don't understand nothing about it.'

'I understand enough, look here, to know the milk isn't safe and me with young ones to feed and all.'

'That's just a lot of crap that is. Propaganda, that's all. Where's that tea, then, Bron? We're thirsty, we are.'

'All right, coming up. Won't be a minute.'

'Did you know old Jones the Post Office had to pay to put new floorboards all over his parlour, Bron? Belly-aching like mad he was.'

'Oh, no I never heard. Why did he?'

'Woodworm in the furniture and they ate their way into the boards and old Mrs Jones, you know what a weight she is, she went in the parlour the other night and damn if the boards didn't give under her. Nearly broke her leg there, they say.' Dai prayed he sounded casual enough and convincing.

'Aye, terrible things, woodworm. They'll eat the house up if you give them half a chance.' Jim looked concerned and turned to assess his wife. 'What's your weight now, Bron? Sixteen stone last time, wasn't it?'

'Oh, no, you don't, Jim Davies Kremlin, not on your Nelly. Woodworm or no, you're not getting my mother's chairs. Don't hope, good boy, give up; you've had it. You won't get them if I have to lock the parlour and sit on the chairs. Beat it, the game's up.'

'Come on, Bron, they're rotten with worm, mun; they wouldn't hold you if you did go and sit on them.'

'Give you one of my chairs and break the set? What a hope, boyo, what a bloody hope.'

'What about the other one? The old one of your grandfather's – that's not a set. Did you know, Dai, that Bron's grandfather was a bard? Aye, indeed, we got this chair upstairs with his name on it – bardic chair from Tumble, 1908 wasn't it, Bron? Clever old boy he was, all right. Bron can be proud of her family indeed.'

'Was he, Bron? I never heard it, look, and me living here all my days.'

'Show Dai the chair, Bron, for him to see. Go on, take him up, I won't be jealous.'

'Yes, show us the chair, girl, I've never seen one close to, never.'

'All right, then, come on up. The kettle will be boiled when we come down.'

'I might as well come too, I know old Dai by there.'

'Nervous, is it, Jim?'

Bron trundled her sixteen stone up the stairs with the two men trailing behind and took them to a small bedroom, with room only for a single bed, a wobbly, bamboo bedside table and the Chair. Made of light, fumed oak and elaborately carved with a rampant dragon resting a cruel, very wooden claw on 'Tumble, 1908', the chair stood four-square in the window, a noble, huge throne, very like a closet-stool, but less utilitarian.

'Well, well,' Dai said from the doorway, 'to think this has been here all these years and I never knew. Goes to show, doesn't it?'

'Go in mun Dai, have a good look, hand-carving look. Solid oak. See the work on it?' Jim tilted the chair and gave a gentle kick to the near back leg. A shower of fine dust cascaded down. 'See that, our Bron, see that dust? There's your worms for you.'

'Leave it alone, you.'

'Aye, lovely chair all right; pity you let it go like this, though, Bron. Look here, look at them holes; it's riddled with you, riddled.'

'Mind, let me see, I can't see no holes.'

'Here, I'll get you your reading glasses; they're in our room since you was reading in bed last night.'

'Try mine, Bron. Fit you all right?'

'Aye, they'll do. Now where's these holes?'

'By here, look.' Dai wrenched the chair up firmly by the other back leg and the leg came off in his hand. 'Oh, my God,' he said, 'that's done it. Sorry, Bron. I didn't mean it, honest. But look, it's rotten, see, gone. Look, you can crumble it in between your fingers.'

Bron slumped down on the single bed. 'My grandfather's chair. My mother'd turn in her grave to see it. Kept it all these years, I have. I wanted the children to have it after me.' The tears in her eyes were enormous under Dai's magnifying lenses. 'Oh, damn you two, what did you want to come pestering me for? Take it, take it away and leave me in peace, you old Bolshies, you thiefs, you. Get out of my house, go on, the two of you. Scram. Get out. Get out, before I crown you. You old devils of hell.'

'Give me my glasses then, Bron, can't see to read much without them.'

'You can rob great without them, whatever. Here, take them. You'll see more than you'll get, no doubt. Let's hope you break your necks on the bloody stairs.'

Silent in victory, they shuffled downstairs carrying the great chair between them. The kettle was boiling its bottom out in the kitchen and Jim made a quick cup of tea for Bron.

'Keep her sweet, Dai boy, keep her sweet. But be ready to sound the retreat.' Jim went to the bottom of the stairs and shouted 'Bron, we've made a cup of tea; Dai and me is off. Have it before it's cold.'

'Good riddance.'

'So long, then.'

No answer.

'Come on, boy, let's go while the going's good. I'll leave a fag in the saucer for her. Peace offerin'.'

CHAPTER 15

Lighting-up time was fixed for eight o'clock, but darkness was pitch-deep by six. Wilf, Geraint, Sam, Iorwerth and Islwyn had been able to hand over five shillings and ninepence, gathered from various more or less legitimate sources, to the Italian, and now Wilf was nursing a box that had contained Plush Nuggets in its sugary prime and was now half-full of bangers, jumpers, atom bombs, golden rain, sparklers and one triumphant, treasure-trove rocket.

Burns notwithstanding, Wilf lit their private bonfire in Sam's garden with wood and kindling stolen from Krem's stores. When the fire was whooping and spitting at them, they padded around it, Indian-style, in their Wellington boots, their faces blackened, old hats of their fathers' drowning their heads, red mouths painted with some mother's stolen lipstick and big brothers' or sisters' coats flopping about their ankles. Drunk with his bonfire, Wilf was the first to go mad. He broke from the Indian file and slipped quietly to the precious box. With shaking fingers, he lit the touch paper of the first atom bomb. There was a silence all about him, a private silence; he watched the small red eye of light creep along the touch paper, he was the light, his whole soul centred on the little light, a little light, then a little fizzle and then a great glory, a roaring, great glory, pretty, nice. Wilf wasn't allowed to get away with that. The others tore to the box like wolves, lighting, lighting, lighting. The rocket went sweeping up the night, the night went wild, fire and beauty and wonder and heaven on earth – and the box was empty.

They threw the box on the fire and the sugar in it sizzled and spat at them and they stood still and they watched and their faces were hot, their eyes smarted and the flames told

lies about castles and caverns and dragons and dares. Wilf
kicked a branch into sparks and there was a nasty smell of
smouldering rubber. They stood, still small statues, and
stared and worshipped; still, absorbed, like broody hens.

Their fire was finished, the glory was gone, and there was
all night to wait before the big fire began. In their Guy
Fawkes' clothes and make-up, it wasn't possible to pursue
their usual ploys – you never saw a cowboy in a bowler, nor
a Jap in a long, long coat.

Tentatively, behind his glasses, Geraint said, 'Why don't
we have a concert now?'

Groans all round.

'No, listen I don't mean singing and that girls' stuff. Let's
have a drama, 'cos we're dressed up ready, is it?'

'All right, we'll have a murder. I'm the judge.'

'I'm the jury.'

'You can't all be the jury. There's got to be the murderer
and the policeman.'

'Well, I'm too small to be a policeman so I'm the jury.'

'Who's the murder going to be, then?'

'Christie?'

'No, that's been done, mun. I know, we'll do Link. You be
the murder, Geraint, you be Link, and then I'll be the judge.
And you be the policemen guarding him and you shall hang
him after. It's not breaking a promise to do it in a drama by
ourselves.'

'O.K. Come on, where's the jail?'

'By here. That corner's the jail. You two grab Link and put
him in jail. Wilf, you be by there, you're the jury. I'll be the
judge, on this pile of small coal.' Sam worked his bottom into
the coal-dust, pulled Geraint's glasses down to the end of his
nose and shouted, 'Bring in the prisoner. Come on, you, you
got to do what the judge tells you.'

'Wait a minute, mun Sam, Ger can't do Link with his coat
on. Half a sec. Right. Come on, you old murder, come on,

quick march, left, right.' In the dim lights from the street lamps and the lighted windows and other, remoter bonfires, Geraint sloped over from the jail with his gorilla walk, his knees bent, his arms trailing and his face creased in malignancy, the two policemen's hands clamped firmly on his shoulders.

'What's your name?' the judge bellowed.

'Link.'

'Where d'you live?'

'In Cilhendre, Glamorganshire, Wales, Great Britain, The World.'

'Did you kill Joe? Guilty or not guilty?'

'Not guilty, what the hell.'

'Liar,' screamed the jury.

'Who's a liar? You mind your own business, see? This is between me and the judge by there.'

'Policemen, is Link guilty?'

'Yes, judge. We was watching him going up the mountain in the morning. He went up to kill Joe.'

'No I never. I never killed Joe. I was going for a walk – it's a free country, isn't it? Who's going to stop me going for a walk if I want?'

A disused siding ran behind the gardens of Railway Street and Link was walking home along the track. He was in a swaggering, devil-may-care mood, having set his teeth to join in the bonfire celebrations and face out the whisperings and damn their eyes, strong in the belief that he was safe, that nobody could prove anything. A few drinks at the Lion had buttressed his courage and his thoughts were full of Cynthia and how he would talk to her, what he'd say. He saw the children in Steve Williams' garden and Geraint's gorilla stroll took him back, like that, to his taunted, persecuted, ridiculed school-days. He stopped in the darkness of the old line and listened and heard the hated, bitten-down, studiously ignored, searing nickname. He stayed in the shadows and watched.

The judge said, 'You wouldn't go for a walk up the mountain for nothing. Nobody'd be so daft. You went up there to kill Joe.'

'Yes, you did, you old liar,' piped the jury.

'Wilf, you got to play right. The jury's not supposed to be buttin' in, is he, Sam?'

'I want a part, don' I? If I don't say nothing, I won't be in the drama. I'm not sittin' here like a mut, come you, and you all talking fifty to the dozen. Not on your Nelly, I'm not.'

The judge cleared his throat, 'Jury, is the prisoner guilty?'

'Of course he's guilty. We can't hang him if he's not, mun.'

'Link, the jury says you're guilty, and the policemen, don't you?'

'Yes,' they snapped their verdict out short, like those in authority.

'So do I; we'll hang you now. Come on, tie him up, policemen.'

'Anybody got a bit of cord?'

The bravado ran out of Link like sweat. Fear trembled through him and hate. He'd kill those bloody kids, get rid of them, murder the little bastards. No respect for their elders, taking a man's character like that. They couldn't have seen him up the mountain; they'd made it up, bloody little liars. Had they told anybody they'd seen him? Couldn't have, or he'd have heard it. He wanted to destroy them, shatter their child voices, stamp down their accusations. How could he do it? Five kids, he hadn't a chance. Threaten them? Frighten the life out of them? They were hanging him now on the apple tree in Steve's garden. They could hang him if they talked, the bloody little liars.

Geraint, with his feet firmly on the ground, held his head on one side, his tongue hanging out, and the others danced around the tree in their floppy long coats and bowler hats, singing,

'We'll hang old Link Davies on the sour apple tree, the sour apple tree . . .'

Something cringed in Link; he wanted to cry, to beg them, to ask for mercy. He hadn't meant to do it, honest to God, he hadn't meant. He was only looking after the horses; nobody cared about the horses but him, and Thunder with a cut on his back as well. He didn't mean it, and how was he to know that Joe was firing? What have I done to deserve this? I never meant no harm. Oh, God, shut their bloody mouths for them, what can I do? Could talk nice to them, give them some fire-works, aye, give them some fireworks. I still got those sticks of gelignite I stole from old Ben. If I put the gel. in with the fireworks? I'll go to the Italian to buy some now. He'll wonder at me buying fireworks; I'll tell him I'm treating the street. For the big bonfire, I'll say. Plenty of accidents with fireworks. No harm in trying. I better hurry to catch them before the big fire. Aye, I'll do it, too. He shambled back to the lighted shops, to the Italian's by the Square.

Geraint grew tired of being hanged after a while. 'Come on,' he cried, 'let's bury me. We'll have a funeral. You'll have to carry me.'

'Who, us? Carry you? No fear, boyo, you can walk. They don't carry murderers.'

'Hey, what's the time, I wonder. Must be nearly time for the fire, must be eight or more.'

'We better ask your mother, Sam, not to be late.'

'Our Mam, what's the time? Time to go to the fire yet?'

'No, it's only quarter past seven. Go and play for a bit again.'

'Can we have something to eat? Got any apples?'

'Pest. Here you are, go now, and don't bother me for a bit; I got to dress your father up and make my lot of chips.'

'Thanks, Mam, mun. See you later, is it?'

'Behave yourselves now, mind you.'

CHAPTER 16

Old Enoch, Chairman of the Cilhendre Old Age Pensioners' Club, was standing guard over the bonfire and the fireworks by the light of six guttering candles stuck into beer bottles and set in a row on the ground. Krem, dressed in the uniform of a French sailor he'd once bought by accident in a jumble sale and wore regularly for Guy Fawkes', was sitting on one of the cases of beer. Beside him on the ground was a large bird-cage containing a brilliant stuffed parrot, which, with the years, had become part of his uniform. He'd acquired a moustache and side-burns since tea-time and was practising his bit of French. 'You like kiss, yes? *Cherchez la femme*,' spoken in the accent of Cilhendre atte Tawe. Dai Dialectic had given himself rosy cheeks and a fat belly, but Enoch was his usual, unprepossessing self. He was a virile old man, given to committees and protests and epically ugly, with a huge nose that went flat and round at the bottom like the bill of a platypus, and his ears stuck out like the doors of a cab. He was lame in one leg with arthritis and he stood beside the preparations with his weight thrown on to one leg and his hand resting on the sore hip. It was to be his privilege as the oldest inhabitant of Railway Street to set the bonfire alight.

'Old Joe would be enjoying this, Krem, wouldn't he, poor fellow? And my old missus too. She was here last year, remember? Making the chips and enjoying herself, God help her. I misses her, Krem, indeed I do.'

'Buried three wives now, haven't you, Enoch?'

'Aye, outlived them all. But it's hard doing without a woman. I'll have to get another one, see. I been looking round, but there's not one I fancy about the place. I can do without my fags, if I got to – do without my beer, at a pinch – but I got to have a woman, honest.'

'For shame on you, Enoch, you're an old man now.'

'Me? Me old? A man's as old as he feels, boyo, but I'll be glad to light this old fire, no mistake, not half cold, is it?'

'You ought to have your overcoat on tonight. You'll catch your death.'

'I don't wear no overcoat till Christmas. Scarf, all right, and a bit of red flannel on my chest, but no overcoat. I'm tough, I am. There's no spunk in you young fellows no more. Seventy-nine I'll be next birthday, and look at me – there's a man for you. Crack nuts with my teeth and read without glasses. I'm great, I am.'

Gradually the people came in from the darkness, most of them wearing some rudimentary disguise, glasses or moustaches, funny hats or pink cheeks, rare enough among colliers to qualify as a disguise. Mrs Link, pathetically eager to be liked, to get back among them, came early, with a steaming shopping basket on her arm, the delicious smell of chips and vinegar like a halo around her.

'Look, Krem,' she said, huge as a double-decker in a flowered, cross-over pinnie, 'I brought my chips early; warm people up while they wait.'

'Oh, lovely, Nell, smashing, girl. Give us a packet to warm my hands. 'S cold out here. Salt and vinegar on ready, is it?'

'Yes, I hope there's enough on them. Shall I give them out, then?'

'I'll do it if you like, Nell.' Dai took the basket and passed out the warm greasy newspaper packets. 'Champion, Nelly, champion. Good timing that was, wasn't it, Enoch?'

'Aye, good girl, Nell. You're getting awful fat, girl. Too many chips, see. How's Tom there?'

'All right, thanks, Enoch. How you keeping?'

'Like I was telling these boys, Nell, I'm great, I am. Is it nearly time to light this bloody fire? I'm cold. Not a night to be out in nothing but your garters, is it, Nell?'

'Here you are, Enoch, have a bottle of beer with your chips. You ought to have your coat on, honest; you haven't even got a muffler on, mun. It's only ten to eight, look, why don't you go home for a scarf, whatever?'

'You won't light it without me then, if I go, will you?'

'Don't be daft, Enoch, you're the official lighter, mun; we'll wait for you, honest.'

'All right, then. It is a cold one, indeed. Won't be long. I'll finish my beer first though. Hahh, that was all right, Krem, lovely. See you later, then.'

The crowd was gathering now, ribald and raucous, in the dark beyond the lights of the six dancing candles; mothers with babies peeping wide-eyed and cheeky from the shawls, girls from the grammar with tunics and long lovely legs and smiles like kittens for the narrow boys with legs like bandy tongs in blue jeans and bum-freezer jackets. The kids were hopping underfoot like sand fleas, wolfing chips and trying to steal bits of the bonfire or a neglected firework.

There were only a few minutes left to zero hour. Enoch's great moment was almost due, but he was still away, making his first concession to the cold. A hush fell over the crowd when Jim Kremlin was seen staggering under the weight of the guy and then carefully climbing up the structure of the fire to put the guy on his high throne. Krem had delayed until the last moment before putting up the guy, for on its chest he had pinned a large cardboard notice which read 'Harold Macmillan' and he was sure that some godforsaken Liberal or a chapel deacon would make him remove his notice if they got a chance. A mixed roar of cheers and boos went up when the crowd saw the guy's name, but it was too late then; Krem had won. He was very delicately balanced on the top of the pile, and the crowd held its breath for him, but Krem was a perfectionist and insisted on giving the hat a final pat and the moustache a last drop of spit, then he waved in shaky triumph and got a shout of approval from below.

Meanwhile, the German engineers, invited in a moment of drunken camaraderie, had turned up punctiliously at eight o'clock. They knew nothing of Enoch and his moment, his Old Age privileges, his sense of occasion. It was eight o'clock and they had arrived; they were gay and were guests and it was time to light the fire. One of them took matches and set alight a letter from his pocket and tossed it on to the paraffin-soaked twigs and newspapers.

The flames scorched up to the night just as Enoch appeared, mufflered, for the consummation. When he saw the flames, his old face puckered like a child's, like an old man's, the tears came to his pale, harmless blue eyes and then his temper took over. 'Damn,' he bawled, 'who done it? Who's the rodney lit the fire? Come on, come out. I may be a old man but I still got a punch or two left. Come on, light the fire when my back was turned, is it? Who sent me home? You, Jim bloody Kremlin. You waster, you, you done it. Where are you? Come out and fight like a man.' He gibbered on his aged feet and feinted with both fists. 'Coward, come on out.' But there was no sign of Jim.

Bron remembered that he'd last been seen on the top of the fire.

'Hey, where's Jim? Dai, where's Jim?' her voice went small and frightened. 'Jim, boy, answer me, where are you? Jim, oh Jim.' She turned on Herr Sprotte. 'Oh, you old Nazi, you've killed my Jim. He was on top of the fire, you bloody fool, he was up there and you lit it. Oh, God in heaven, Dai mun, where's Jim? Burnt to a cinder he'll be. Put it out, for God's sake, do something. They did it, those old Germans – not enough to kill young Joe for his girlfriend, they got to burn my Jim. Damn you, Dai, put this bloody fire out. Who asked these old foreigners to come here, anyway? Who asked you, I'd like to know? Fetch water, go on, run, fetch water to

dout it in the name of God.' But most of the spectators were
deaf in the roar of the flames and the wonder and splendour
of the great burst. Enoch was still dancing on his toes in
impotent rage; now he wanted to take on all the Germans for
lighting his fire. Mrs Krem's friends gathered around her
adding their mite to the attack. 'Yes, somebody fetch water,
quick. Coming here, killing everybody.' Water, water, the cry
went up from Mrs Krem's side of the fire; Link heard the
shout and ran to the nearest house for buckets, determined to
prove. He had been to the Italian's shop, but the Italian was
sold out; not a squib was left, not even a box of magnesium
matches. Every firework in Cilhendre was sold. Link had
stared at the handsome, warm-eyed, shrugging Italian. 'Got
some under the counter for your pals, I bet.'

'No, Tom, not one is left. Look, see, nothing. Good business. Very fine.' He grinned his flash of teeth at Link, but
Link had only kicked open the shop door and let it thump
behind him. Then a kind of lethargy had come over him, an
acceptance. Oh, what could he do? Only hope and watch and
deny everything. They wouldn't believe kids before him,
would they, for God's sake? He'd go to the Lion again and
then face them after.

So he ran for the water and bumped slap into Joe Kremlin
coming from behind a shed. 'Krem, boy, Krem, we thought
you was burned, your missus said you was on top of the fire.'

'Who, me? Who'd you think I am, a bloody witch? I was
only opening my trousers behind the shed. Can't a man have
a quiet one no more without everybody thinking he's dead?'

'Well, you better hurry to tell them or your missus will
pull the fire to pieces.'

'What, spoil my fire? I'll give her fire, mind – get out of
my way. Spoil my fire would she?' He ran up to where Bron
was screaming and, standing behind her, clapped his hands
over her eyes and shouted, 'Boo!' in her ear. She spun round
at him, 'Oh, you devil, you. I thought you was dead.'

'Well, I'm not, see. Disappointed, is it?'

Mrs Link was delighted to have discovered new suspects for Joe's accident and took up the battle against the Germans who were standing in a bewildered, unhappy knot while Enoch, like an enraged bantam rooster, tried to take them all on. Nell Link waddled into the engagement like a floral sow. 'Enoch had the privilege of lighting this fire. Oldest inhabitant he is, you had no business. Who d'you think you are, after all?' But Steve Williams came up before she could bring out her guns. Steve was wheezing in his Home Guard uniform and an undertaker's top-hat.

'Shut up, Nell. Shut your mouth now, before you say something you'll be sorry for.' She recognised something in the glint of his one good eye that went through her like a hot knife into butter, like a purge, like a burn, and she backed away, to lose herself among the other women.

'Sorry about that bit of misunderstanding gents,' Steve said to the engineers. 'Here, have a bottle of beer each and here's some chips in this basket, look. Make yourselves at home. Come on, Enoch, here's your bottle, look. The gentlemen made a mistake; no offence meant, none taken. We'll drink to the health of Enoch, the man who's going to live to be a hundred and ten – that right, Enoch, boy? Look, Enoch, I've got the rockets by here, I want you to send them off – send up half a dozen one after another. Here's the matches. One, two, three, go, for everybody to know Railway Street is off. Right?'

'Shall I, Steve? Right, boys, right. Finish my bottle first, is it? Now then, let's have them matches and room to move here. Start counting down, you blokes, to see if you know a bit of English. Go on, ten, nine, eight – like that.' Enoch crouched over the row of rockets like Hardy's ageing thrush, his left hand resting on the pain in his hip, and a long taper in his eager, trembling, old right hand.

As the rockets hissed their flash of glory into the throbbing night, Steve was suddenly aware of Bryn and Flossie standing momentarily in the glare. They stood arm-in-arm, she leaning into him, on to his strength, clinging to him and turning her face up to say some word to him. They looked like refugees, lost, incongruous, biblical, underlining their exile in their little joining, their gesture of approval. Steve wanted them to go away; their bravery was agonising to him, like fire on his flesh, churning his guts, but he couldn't look away, he watched it out. They stood a while, and Flossie nodded and smiled and then Steve saw Bryn speak to her and they turned away and he was leading her, guiding her, as a man might prop, support, his mother.

Steve was glad when they went. He self-consciously shook off, put aside, the sadness they had engendered, the depression, the sick despair, and set his undertaker's hat at a firmer angle. Enoch and the Germans were now fast friends; he was telling them what a great man he was and distributing fireworks with wicked abandon. The beer and the elderberry wine flowed, the chips were warm and delicious and the fire roared in primeval ecstasy. The bardic chair blazed up and Krem shouted, 'Hark at the woodworms poppin',' and Bron shouted back, 'You wait till I catch you, boy.'

Still the guy rode triumphant on the crest, then the heavy chair settled, sank, and he was up and away and Jim Whitmarsh's suit had had its best day. Then Krem and Dai Dialectic stood together, bare-headed, struck a Napoleonic pose, one in French naval uniform, the other with a capitalist's belly and rosy cheeks, and sang together 'The Red Flag'. The crowd joined in at the chorus, the older, fat mothers waving their hands in the air at 'raise the scarlet standard high', despite the fact that their revolutionary fervour was about equal to that of the man whose effigy they had just burned. The Germans sang then 'O Tannenbaum' and Krem went crazy with delight, for he thought they were singing his song, the workers of the world were uniting under his very nose. From the women's side of the fire a soprano voice

struck up 'Aberystwyth', and Railway Street sang like
angels, sang in their disguises, smelling of chips and beer,
sang out of the darkness, around the flames. Steve conduct-
ed with his top-hat. He saw Link singing with the best of
them, his inevitable compassion took over and, as the last
repeated chorus hung in the air, Steve drew Link towards him
and whispered in his ear. Into the silence, Link, hideous as
ever, but in the merciful shadows, sang in his bass-baritone,
'Oh, I do love my boss, he's a great pal of mine', the street
responded with 'Halleluja, I'm a bum' and then Steve took
up the next verse in his breathless tenor, his arm over Link's
shoulder, 'Why don't you work, like other men do?' and Link
roared, 'How the hell can I work, when there's no work to
do?' Steve's gesture put Link right back among them; Link
was right, God help him, and Mrs Link moved a bit closer to
the fire.

The beer had run out and the chip papers had all been
burned when Krem passed around a quiet word at there was
only half an hour to stop-tap at the The Lion. The drinkers
slowly melted from the scene and left the dying embers to the
intoxicated kids, the posturing adolescents and the mothers.

Krem was full. The German engineers had stood whisky all
round when they got to the Lion and the whisky soured
Krem. 'Damn,' he said – suddenly, abruptly, fighting-drunk.
'Damn, it's not right. Old Joe. Old Joe's not here. And who'd
have been the life and soul of it tonight? I ask you. Joe. Joe'd
have been – Joe was the best boy in this village. And where
is he? I ask you, where is he? Gone. Gone to pay for coal –
coal for the bloody capitalist class. Who was he? One of the
factors of production; expendable, just overheads. What's
life to them, the bastards? Nothing; expendable, that's what
he was, our Joe. God, if I could find the bastard killed him,
I'd scrag him with my bare hands, indeed to God I would.
Accidental death, they said. Accident my arse. Murdered he

was, murdered by the capitalist class or some other bugger.'
He was standing now, holding up his glass with the last drops
of whisky golden in the bottom, and rocking on drunken feet.
'What am I drinking, boys? Look at me, drinking whisky.
Where's my shame? So much for whisky' – and he turned his
glass upside-down and, with glazed eyes, watched the little
pool of liquid spread on the floor. Then he spat at the pool, in
his naval uniform, with his parrot cage dangling from his left
hand; staggered against the tables, trying to balance on his
heels.

'Who killed Joe, I want to know; who killed him? Capital
murder it was, death by explosion, ought to be hanged.
Ought to swing, by God – be damned to you, Steve
Williams.' He rocked again and then sat down abruptly,
keeping his back straight and his head up, struggling to fix
his eyes. 'Where's Dai? Where's my friend Dai? Come here,
Dai, mun, come here by me.' Dai sat beside him, looking
foolish and tolerant and apologetic and loyal all at the same
time. 'Here I am, Krem.'

'Dai, you're a pal, you know that? The best pal a man
ever had. We made a good old fire, di'n we, Dai mun.
Lovely fire.' Krem put his arm around Dai's shoulder and
half sang, in a mixture of notes and mumbles, the first bars
of the 'Internationale', then he slumped all over Dai and
rested his face in a pool of spilt beer on the table beside
him.

Steve had watched Link's face during Krem's perform-
ance; the habitual expression of stupid, wooden, animal puz-
zlement didn't change. It was not a collapse, a decay, of
expression that Steve witnessed, suffered, felt for, but the
change that came over the clay of his face, the underground
pallor turning dead, bleached and dry like an old grey bone,
the bristles standing harsh and dark. The poor devil's afraid;
afraid they'll hang him, afraid we'll all know, turn our backs.
What can I say to him, how can I save him, give him a leg

up? That Krem's a bloody fool, I wish he'd shut his mouth. Keep cool now, Link, ride it out, you're doing fine, nobody's looking at you, keep it up.

Steve turned to the Germans with a great tolerant laugh, his hand resting lightly, in a kind of silent apology, on Krem's unconscious French hat, 'Krem can see the dead hand of capitalism everywhere. He's a great old Bolshie, Krem is, and he's got this daft notion from somewhere that Joe's death wasn't accidental. But they've had an Enquiry and the verdict was accidental death, I don't know what he's blathering about– It touched his pocket, see, he had to go cap in hand to the Coal Board to get another job when they closed the small mine and it's hurt his pride, that's all. There's no harm in old Krem, he's the right sort. He'd be the first to fight any old Commissar that tried to throw his weight around Cilhendre, believe you me. Much communism in Germany now, with you?'

'More than we like, Steve.'

'Well, you rather have that than the Nazis, I'm sure. I know I would, whatever – no offence, mind you, no offence. Cigarette?'

'Thank you.'

'I see you got old Adenauer back again, then. Good chap, is he?'

'The best, Steve, the best.'

'Well, here's to him, then, good luck to him if he's making a tidy job of things and keeping the old Nazis out. Here, have one of mine, Tom, you only got that one left.' Steve saw Link having to swallow before he got his voice out to say, 'Ta, Steve,' and he was reminded again of how men's Adam apples let them down. Steve had once been a witness in an accident case in the court and, sitting through the earlier cases, with a clear view of the accused up there above him, naked to the public eyes, he'd watched their throats as they spoke or waited or were shamed and had seen the pathetic workings of the naked Adam's apples, revealing, telling, while the faces were held, frozen, stiff.

'Drink up, gentlemen, last orders, please.' The Germans put up whiskies again, but Krem didn't come round to drink his and so betray his working-class principles. Dai and Sam, the landlord, stretched him out on a bench in the bar, threw an old coat over him and left him there to sleep, with his faithful parrot at his feet.

Steve walked home with Link. They set off in silence. Link was never a talker, even in drink, and Steve was rehearsing what he thought he'd better say. The lights of dying bonfires still lit the sky and the tips and mountains in the dark seemed to have crowded in closer, nearer, a black circle, embracing.

'Tom,' he said at last, 'don't be afraid of what Krem was saying in by there. Don't worry about it.'

'Afraid? What the hell d'you mean, Steve Williams?'

'You know what I mean all right, Tom. Look, let's tell the truth about this, once and for all, and then finish; have it out.'

'Have what out?'

They paused in the dark, the two of them, on the pavement, and watched the last bus pass down the valley. In spite of Link's denials, there was an underlying, unexpressed acceptance of the truth between them.

'There's no need to say it, better not to say things in so many words, but I know you was there that Sunday morning. You was seen, Tom boy. And I know you wouldn't have harmed Joe for the world, but we know those sprags were safe Saturday. Right, then. Now what we've got to do is learn to live with this; not only you, me too. I was fond of Joe, and Bryn is a pal of mine, see, and you are too. I'm not saying you and me's been as close as I've been to Bryn, but we've got to live here together, you and me, and to tell the truth, Tom, I wants to help you.'

'I don't need no help. I got nothing to worry about.'

'Oh, God, Tom, you have – we both know you have, mun, let's quit all this cackling. What I want to say is, don't be afraid. I was watching you in there tonight and you was scared. I saw it, mun, but don't be afraid. The question is closed; accidental death it was, and there's no doubt about that; of course it was accidental so stop being frightened. See, fear is so bad for you. Fear harms you inside, distorts you; d'you know what I mean now, Tom? Fear changes you, like, so that you don't know yourself, makes you do things you'd be ashamed of, makes you warped – you know, mun, like a horse underground, you can't do nothing with it if it's frightened. You got to handle it right. The best horse is unmanageable if you frighten it, right?'

'Aye.'

'Well there you are. So don't be frightened no more. There's no need, believe me, not to be frightened. Mind, you can have something on your conscience all right, it's you's got to live with that; but, see, there's no room to have it on your conscience, no time, if you're all filled up with fear. The old fear will make you feel that you're O.K. with your conscience, like – as if you're paying – and you wouldn't want that, would you?'

'I don't know what you're talking about.'

'All right, then, you don't know what I'm talking about. O.K. All I'm saying is, don't be afraid. We'll drop the subject. I'm home, anyway. We'll forget all about this little conversation, except to say one last thing, Tom; the kids, my Sam and those, were the ones saw you, and they won't say anything. They've given their words. So, like I said, don't worry no more about Krem and that. Good night, then.' Steve turned in at his front gate and Link walked on without a word.

Why didn't I give the swine a shove under that bus? I could have said he was drunk and slipped. Who does he think he is, preaching at me? He always was an interfering devil;

why can't he mind his own damn business? Calling me his pal, not half! I got no pals, don't want them – interfering in a man's private affairs. I wonder if it's true about those kids not splitting; kids forget things quick . . . but what the hell, who'd believe a gang of kids like that, taking a man's character and all? And I never meant it, see, I never meant no harm to him. What would she say if she knew, wouldn't have a word for me then, I bet. What was that he said about fear changing a bloke? P'raps he's got something there. Aye. I wouldn't have thought about them fireworks if I hadn't been scared of the kids, nor the bus neither. Not before this, I wouldn't; no, I'm sure I wouldn't. Well if he is right they won't say, there's nothing to worry about, is there? It was only drink talking in Krem, forget it. Best of it is, I didn't mean to do it, I never meant no harm, I wouldn't have done it, I'm sure I wouldn't have done it, I didn't know, see, only did it to spite old Ben Butch. He's had his chips now, too; working in Cefn Coed, nobody's boss no more. I hope the horses like their new place.

He came to his own house and in at the back door. His wife, knitting a vast purple jumper, was waiting for him, and his supper was ready on the table, timed for stop-tap.

'You're back, then.'

'No, I'm still in the Lion.'

'The fire went all right, didn't it?'

He didn't answer, but sat at the table waiting for her to serve him. Before she poured his tea, he peered inside the cup to make sure that it was clean, then he took the corner of the table-cloth and wiped his plate over, passed the cloth through the prongs of his fork and wiped his knife. Of such small insults was their life compounded; his attitudes towards her were habitual, patterned; tenderness from him would be painfully embarrassing to both, gentleness would be indecent exposure.

'Any news in the Lion, Tom?'

'No.'

'Anybody say anything to you?'

'What d'you mean, say anything? Think they've gone dumb there?'

'No, I was only asking.'

'Shut your mouth, then, if you can't talk sense.'

She picked up her knitting again and quietly hummed to herself, 'Jesus knows all about my troubles'. He looked at her from under his low brow, without lifting his head from over his plate, 'Garn,' he snarled, and putting on a falsetto voice he sang a depravity of her comfort, 'There's not a friend like the lowly Jesus no not one, no not one,' pulling grotesque faces and finally putting out his tongue at her, covered as it was with half-chewed food. The silence fell again and she waited, passive and submissive, until he had finished his meal and slumped off to bed, leaving her to wash up and prepare the breakfast table and bank the fire and set the alarm for six o'clock, when she would be up again to see him safely off to work.

'Don't be long down there,' he shouted over the banisters, 'I'm waiting.'

CHAPTER 17

There was small boy in an orphanage once who thought that Christmas was an orange, but in Cynthia's mother's shop Christmas was a box. Halfway through November Mrs Griffiths had heard the herald angels and the message they gave her was 'boxes'. She boxed her handkerchiefs, her stockings, her scarves, her blouses, her jewellery and labelled them 'Artistic' or 'Suitable Gift' or 'For Him' or 'Seasonable'. Over all she sprinkled synthetic flakes, called glitter; this got into her hair and into her mouth and stuck to the point of her pen, and every mat in the house was wearing sparklers.

Mrs Griffiths aggravated the problems of glitter by breathing gusty sighs over her boxes and working up small sandstorms of distress. Cynthia had decided that she must leave home, had applied for a transfer to a Coal Board office in the Midlands, and the kindly Area General Manager had arranged it for her. 'Get out of it lass,' he'd said; 'cut your losses;' and now she was to go, to leave home for the first time, to leave her mother, to leave her alone with nothing but the accounts for company in the long evenings. 'Oh, dear, dear,' Mrs Griffiths reiterated, and was sick of Christmas before the end of November.

Lil Cream Slices came to sympathise and to glean. 'Cyn's going away, then?'

'Yes. She knows what's best, I suppose. I wouldn't stand in her way.'

'She'll be homesick in England, won't she? All that way. You'll miss her, Mrs Griffiths.'

'Oh, Lil, don't talk. I can't tell you.'

'She's young, too. Going to live in lodgings, is it?'

'Yes, the AGM recommended her to a place; he's from those parts himself. He's been very good to her. I must give him that.'

'Why does she want to leave you, then?'

'Wants a change, she says. She hasn't got over – you know, the old trouble – only she won't say. I think she wants to see new faces and that. Everything reminds her down here. It'll be different in England and I'm hoping she'll meet some nice young fellow there. She doesn't go out with anybody now, see, Lil. There's that nice young German – she won't have anything to do with him, she says it's too embarrassing. And I think people are shy to ask her, for a start.'

'She wouldn't like to go about with girls; I can understand that, too, can't you? Girls are awful insipid once you've started courting. God help her, too.'

'But she won't talk about it still, see. Bites your head off if you try to say something tactful, like. So I'm saying, she can go if she wants. If it helps her. The change will be good for her.'

'She won't find anybody else as good as her mother to her, Mrs Griffiths fach. Pity she's going before Christmas.'

'She's coming back for the holidays, of course.'

'Oh, yes, that'll be nice for you.'

'Don't say anything, but I think there's an old chap down the colliery who's getting on her nerves a bit, too. Some old fellow that knew Joe. He's always hanging around her, never saying much – just looks at her and hangs about her. He's so ugly and pathetic-looking, Cyn said, she hasn't got the heart to cut him. But it's getting her down a bit. She'll be glad to get rid of that one.'

'Drop dead! Fancies her, like, does he?'

'No, girl, he's a married man, old enough to be her father; only wants to be friendly, I suppose, because he knew Joe, but it's not nice, hanging about like that and bringing it all back to her.'

'No, indeed. Must be embarrassing for her, too. Well, she knows her own mind. She's got plenty of sense, old Cyn. You've brought her up lovely, fair play.'

'All I want is for her to be happy, Lil; never mind about me being by myself, I'll manage. I've managed worse things. Times like this I miss Gwilym. It's ten years since he passed away, but I miss him – oh, Lil, I miss him! The young ones don't understand.' Mrs Griffiths pushed her handkerchief carefully under her spectacles and delicately wiped her eyes.

'Come you, Mrs Griffiths fach, p'raps she won't like it in England after all. She may be back again in a wink.'

'No, I want her to do what's best. We've got to be brave, haven't we, Lil?'

'It'll be hard on her too, mind you, amongst a lot of strangers. Is there a little Welsh chapel where she's going? They say there's a lot of them in England.'

'To Nottingham she's going. I don't know if there's a chapel there; not that our Cyn goes much, anyway.'

'No; but away from home, it would be company, like. What did you say the place was?'

'Nottingham.'

'Further than London, is it?'

'Oh, yes, beyond Birmingham it is. Did you want something, Lil, or only coming to see me?'

'Well both, to tell the truth. Here's a half-crown, look, put it on my Club Card. I brought it tonight when I had it – if I kept it till tomorrow it would go for sure. How much is on my card now?'

'I'll count it up; wait a minute. That's twelve and six now, Lil.'

'Can't buy much with that, can I? Oh, I fair hates Christmas, honest. Counting and counting and stretching the bit of pay. It's not worth it, Mrs Griffiths, is it? And I never get a present myself. I have to buy something for the old man to give me, not to look small in front of the neighbours. He needs a new shirt bad, but he'll have to wait now to have it for his Christmas-box. When did you say she was going?' Lil directed a breath upwards to blow a piece of glitter off the end of her nose.

'Next Wednesday.'

'Well, come round to our house after she's gone. I'll send the kids to the pictures and he'll be in the pub. I'll ask Mrs Morgans Don't Care in for a cup of tea, is it? We can have a little chat and Mrs Morgans can tell our fortunes. She's good with the tea-cups. Been promising me money for years. I'm still hoping. You never know, there's always the pools. Those pools have done me more good than all the National Health put together, honest; always got something to hope for, see. I know exactly how I'd spend every penny if my number came up. No harm in dreaming, is there? Keeps me going, whatever.'

CHAPTER 18

Link was crouched on his haunches in a tram, his head bowed low, skimming the roof. He was close packed into the corner of the tram with several other colliers all in that same foetal position, heads down like children defaecating. They were riding an empty journey part of the way to the coal face, each with his head turned down and the beam of his light concentrated, sharp, on a spot at his feet, on the colours of the small coal, the dust, the mud-encrusted boots, the rusting cast-iron of the tram. They talked a little over the rattle and jump of the journey on the rails.

'We're in the best place today, boys, with all that rain on top. We got a bit of shelter here, whatever.'

'It rained cats and dogs in the night. Woke me up once. I had to get the missus to close the window.'

'Turned awful hygienic, haven't you? We don't open no windows in our place after October. Blankets is too dear.'

'Oh, I likes a bit of fresh air, but the wife is tamping. She says the curtains have got a tide-mark after the rain. Get very wet coming in?'

'Bit, see. But the clothes will soon dry off in the lockers. Don't half go for my back, this rain. I been rubbing Sloan's in it till most of my skin's off, honest. You'll have to help me out of this tram, boys, indeed to God; I'll never straighten out by myself.'

'O.K. Sloan's, we won't abandon you, never fear. Did you hear young Miss Griffiths is leaving the office? Being moved to Nottingham, I heard. Pity too, she's a nice little thing; I likes to see a pretty girl about the place. No harm to her, mind, but it's nice to see them, like, isn't it? The might-havebeens. Quite satisfied with what I've got, mind you, but you can't help thinking.'

'Aye, she's all right, that one. Going to England, is she? Shows she's got a bit of sense, whatever, it'll take her mind off.'

Link in his corner, his womb, was silent, still; moved, rocked, by the swing of the tram, but holding himself, his reactions, his control, tight and reined. He showed no interest in the conversation, took no part, but the news of Cynthia's treachery shot through him like a sudden pain, unexpected, taking his breath. She hadn't told him; he was the last to know, like a husband is the last to know of his wife's infidelity.

They came to the end of the line. They clambered over the steep sides of the tram, keeping their heads down from habit.

The man with the back said, 'I'll never make it, boys.'

'Here's a crow-bar, look, shall I lever you out?'

'Don't be daft now, good boy, I can't make it, honest; it's killing me. Jesus!'

'Come here, put your arms round my shoulders, and Jenkin shall push from behind. All right, Jenkin? You get back in the tram and shove. Mind your head, mun. Come on now; one, two, three, shove.'

'Oh, Christ, I'm dying, honest – you'll kill me, you'll break me in half. Oh, thanks, boys. I'll do now, I think, but I'm going sick tomorrow, pay packet or not. Ta.'

Link hadn't offered his help. He walked on, stooping, alone, thinking. He had eventually to crawl on his hands and knees; the plough which, like a dragon, was eating up the face wrenched the coal out and threw it on to the conveyor belt that moved smoothly like a black snake beside Link's face as he went forward, on his knees, sometimes on his belly. He dodged and slipped, slithered, grunted greetings and came at last-breath to the security of his own place, his stall, his sanctuary. But not in the old sense a sanctuary, not as it had been

in his young days, a place of refuge; his own, his own to keep
neat and organised and orderly; this was a sanctuary only in
its darkness, its familiar shape, its aloneness.

He worked his shift doggedly; dodging, ducking, racing to
keep up with the devouring plough, automatic, workmanlike.
His thoughts were his own; no one bothered him, no one
talked; the noise was there, the terrible noise, but he was free
to think quietly. She was going away. She didn't realise. Fair
play, she didn't know. She didn't know about Joe and him –
he hadn't really told her, come to think; she didn't know why
he was so special. Perhaps she wouldn't go if she knew. She
wasn't to go without knowing, for a fact. He'd have to tell
her; fair play, she didn't know. Couldn't blame her, really.
Yes, he'd tell her. Steve Williams said there was no need to
be afraid any more, he could tell her. Be nice to tell her, she'd
understand then; she might even be willing to stay. He'd be
nice to her, make up for it. How could he make up for it?
Him? He couldn't do anything. Make up for it? He hadn't
thought like that before. Make up for it to Bryn and Flossie,
too? What good could he do? He'd done it, hadn't he? God,
yes, but he hadn't meant, he hadn't meant it. God knows he
hadn't meant. God knows. Did God know? 'God can see you,
Tom,' he heard his mother's voice, 'God can see you, God
knows when you're telling lies, God can see you opening my
purse, God knows all about us, it's all written down in God's
book.' Does God know, though? Does God know the
reasons? Did God see him opening his mother's purse to buy
friends, to buy peace, to stop them – the kids in the school-
yard, the taunts, the shame? Did God know he hadn't meant
with Joe? He'd have to prove somehow, show he hadn't
meant. He'd tell her, talk about it. Show her. He'd talk to her
today, after the shift. He'd make her understand; he was only
spiting Ben Butch, he wasn't to know about Joe. Steve
Williams wasn't a bad sort. A pal of mine, he'd said; he
hadn't said any more about that night, the night of the bus

and the bonfire. He seemed to have forgotten. Everybody
seemed to have forgotten. Krem hadn't said any more.
Everybody was forgetting. Except him. And Bryn and
Flossie. And Cynthia. She mustn't forget. She mustn't forget
Joe and him. If she forgot Joe, she'd forget him too; no, she
mustn't forget Joe. Joe was his right to her. He'd talk to her.
Get this shift over and he'd see her; she'd be in the canteen
when he came up, he'd watch for her coming out. Get this
shift over now, quick.

The rain was still sluicing down when he came out of the
lamp-room, bucketing down, and he stood outside the lamp-
room, watching the door of the canteen. There was a little
shelter there, a foot of concrete lintel. He watched the rain
slashing, bouncing big drops in the black puddles, streaming
down the windows of the office, the canteen, the engine
house, moving down the valley like a curtain.

She wouldn't come out till it eased off, he'd have to wait.
He'd lose the bus; never mind, there'd be another one some-
time. She'd have to come soon, she only had a quarter of an
hour for tea; she'd have to come soon for the other girls to
get theirs. No, she wouldn't be long now.

Cynthia had seen Link waiting through the windows of
the canteen and had delayed as long as she could, but he
waited, waited. She wasn't exactly afraid of him, but he
embarrassed her, disconcerted her, made her unsure; he was
like a stray dog that follows one home or an abandoned kitten
that cries to be let in. She didn't want him, she wished he
wasn't there – just wasn't there. But her bags were packed,
she was going away; he wouldn't be in Nottingham. What
the hell, it was all finished, today was the last day. She might
as well go, say good-bye to him, like everything else. The
last cup of tea in the canteen. She was leaving it, cutting her
losses like the AGM had said. Old Tom out there was certainly a loss worth cutting, if ever there was a loss in this world,

God help. She tied on a head-scarf and pulled her coat close. 'Good-bye,' she called to the men there, 'good-bye. I'll come back and see you Christmas time. Be good.'

'So long, Miss Griffiths. Good luck – you'll need it in old England. Keep your end up. Be seeing you.'

'Yes, I'll be back. So long.' She went through the door and he moved across towards her in the cloud-burst rain.

'I heard you was going away.'

'Yes,' she spoke with a bright crispness, 'yes, Mr Davies, I'm off tomorrow.'

'You didn't tell me. Tomorrow?'

'Well it was all rather sudden. I've been transferred to the Nottingham office. Still with the Coal Board, though.'

'I wish you'd told me. I had to hear it from strangers.' His tweed cap was saturated, dark, and drips plopped from the peak of it; she could feel the wet through her head-scarf, it would ruin her set.

'Well, good-bye, Mr Davies, I'll have to run. I mustn't keep the others back and I'll get soaking standing here.'

'No, don't go for a minute. I got to say something to you. I got to talk to you.'

'Well, walk with me as far as the office, then.'

'You didn't ought to go without telling me. See, you – well, I mean, I – well, I took Joe from you; I took him away from you, so, well, we're butties, like, you and me.'

'I don't know what you mean, Mr Davies, and you know I'd rather not talk about – about all that.'

'There's no time now for manners. You got to talk about it. I got to tell you. You got to realise. You know that old journey smashed into him, right? Well, I sent it. I sent the journey down. I didn't know about Joe being there, I only sent the journey because of Ben Butch. Nothing to do with Joe, only Joe was there. So I robbed you, see, didn't I? But I never meant – but I robbed you. I wanted you to know. I was hoping p'raps you'd stay now. I wanted you to stay because

I took Joe from you. That's why I'm somebody special to you, that's why you belong to me – like, well, like a cousin or something; but you mustn't go till I tell you or you won't know about you and me belonging, see.'

'You mean you killed him?' Her voice was quiet, whispering its fear, her scarf was plastered to her head, the rain in dark patches on her shoulders. Her thoughts came in waves, washing over her mind like tides; he's mad, why is he telling me this? He's a murderer, I'm not safe, why does he say I belong to him? I think I'm frightened, he must be mad. I don't believe it, the Enquiry would have found out. He's only saying this to keep me talking, p'raps I ought to tell the police or something.

'But I didn't mean. Accidental it was, accidental.' His face was still stupidly expressionless, but he shook his head, shook his head and then lifted his eyes to look into her face. 'Accidental, honest. I never meant,' the voice hoarse, supplicating.

Again she felt unable to conform to the orthodox reactions, the natural, expected responses; again the reality of her feelings was out of step, incongruous. Here, wet and hideous and meaningless, was the murderer of her hopes – if he was telling the truth – of her hopes, her little dreams, her Joe, her young man. She knew she ought to hit at him, tear him, but all she did was to put her small hand on his sodden sleeve and say, 'No, I'm sure you didn't mean it, whatever it was. I'm sorry.'

'You understand now, then. You realise. You mustn't forget me.'

'Oh, God, no, I'm not likely to forget you now, am I? Why are you doing this?'

'I only want you to realise, that's all.'

She looked into his face again and they were both silent. She was rudderless, young, bewildered, wounded. She wanted to run away, to run home, to get out of it, to step aside from it, but he was there, standing before her in the rain, bedraggled, wet, impossible, inconceivable. Her face was sallow, twisted, bleak, miserable as indigestion. She built up a barricade of words.

'Don't talk about it any more. Don't talk about it, I tell you. You can't bring him back. Don't think about it any more. Finish, finish. No, don't upset yourself. Good-bye now, thank you. We mustn't think about it any more. I'll be back and we'll have a cup of tea, p'raps, together. No, I won't forget you, no. Good-bye.'

She broke away from the stare of his eyes, the pathos of his ugliness. Please, God, save me, don't let me ever see him again. Just let me get away, don't let me think of it, let me forget. She turned from him and ran, refusing, rejecting, torn, frightened, and left him in the rain, there on the top, alone, bowed, shabby, the winding gear behind him, the pipes leaking steam around him and the rain coming crossing down like a curtain.

MORE GREAT NOVELS FROM MENNA GALLIE

You're Welcome to Ulster

Introduction by Claire Connolly, Angela V. John

First published in 1970, this was one of the very first novels confronting the 'Troubles' in Northern Ireland and also reflects the movement towards sexual freedom of the late 1960s.

Sarah Thomas has a life threatening disease and before an important operation she decides that it is time for a holiday, potentially her last, and to revisit old friends and lovers in Ulster. But as well as longed for reunions, her visit brings an unwelcome glimpse into the lives of those for whom politics may come before life itself. Visiting in the July week that sees the county of Ulster become a chain of bonfires and unionist fervour, she finds herself thrust into the midst of a country on the brink of guerrilla war.

£8.99
978-1-906784-19-5

Strike for a Kingdom

Introduction by Angela V. John

First published in 1959, this novel is set in the fictional Valleys town of Cilhendre at the time of the 1926 miners' strike. The murder of a hated mine manager exposes the tensions and secrets of this close knit South Wales community. The book was described by critics at the time as an 'outstanding detective story that is genuinely different' and as a 'poet's novel' despite being a 'whodunnit'. *Strike for a Kingdom* was shortlisted for the CWA gold dagger award.

£8.99

978-1-870206-58-7

All Honno titles are available from good bookstores
and online booksellers.
They can also be ordered online at **www.honno.co.uk**,
with **free** p&p to all UK addresses.

Travels with a Duchess

Introduction by Angela V. John

First published in 1968, the story is set in the sixties during the first days of the 'package' holiday when new horizons were opening up for postwar Brits.

Just how much trouble can a Welsh Shirley Valentine get into on a foreign holiday? On her way to Yugoslavia, Innes Gibson loses her luggage, her patience and her head. She spends the next fortnight trying on a different life as well as another woman's clothes. Reeling from sight to sight, from drink to drink, from man to man, she finds out more about herself in two weeks than in the previous forty years put together. Aided and abetted by the enigmatic Duchess, our heroine returns to Cardiff a little wiser and a lot merrier.

£8.99
978-1-870-206-22-8

All Honno titles are available from good bookstores and online booksellers.
They can also be ordered online at **www.honno.co.uk**, with **free** p&p to all UK addresses.

MORE GREAT CLASSICS FROM HONNO

Honno's Classics are a unique series which bring books by women writers from Wales, long since out of print, to a new generation of readers.

Dew on the Grass
Eiluned Lewis

With a new explanatory introduction by Dr Katie Gramich.
Set in the Welsh borders, this enchanting autobiographical novel vividly evokes the essence of childhood and a vanished way of life. The novel was first published in 1934 to great acclaim.
9781870206808 £8.99

Stranger Within the Gates
Bertha Thomas

Edited by Kirsti Bohata
A collection of witty, sharply observed short stories written at a time of great social change, when the fundamental rights of women were being questioned. Bertha Thomas deftly sketches her characters with a keen eye for satirical details.
9781870206945 £8.99

A View Across the Valley: Short Stories by Women from Wales c. 1850 – 1950
Edited by Jane Aaron

Stories reflecting the realities, dreams and personal images of Wales – from the industrial communities of the south to the hinterlands of the rural west. This rich and diverse collection discovers a lost tradition of English-language short story writing.
9781870206358 £7.95

Queen of the Rushes: A Tale of the Welsh Revival
Allen Raine

First published in 1906 and set at the time of the 1904 Revival. An enthralling tale of complex lives and loves, it will capture the romantic heart of any modern reader.
9781870206297 £7.95

All Honno titles are available from good bookstores and online booksellers.
They can also be ordered online at **www.honno.co.uk**, with **free** p&p to all UK addresses.

ABOUT HONNO

Honno Welsh Women's Press was set up in 1986 by a group of women who felt strongly that women in Wales needed wider opportunities to see their writing in print and to become involved in the publishing process. Our aim is to develop the writing talents of women in Wales, give them new and exciting opportunities to see their work published and often to give them their first 'break' as a writer.

Honno is registered as a community co-operative. Any profit that Honno makes is invested in the publishing programme. Women from Wales and around the world have expressed their support for Honno by buying shares. Supporters liability is limited to the amount invested and each supporter has a vote at the Annual General Meeting.

To buy shares or to receive further information about forthcoming publications, please write to Honno at the address below, or visit our website: www.honno.co.uk.

Honno
Unit 14, Creative Units
Aberystwyth Arts Centre
Penglais Campus
Aberystwyth
Ceredigion
SY23 3GL

All Honno titles can be ordered online at
www.honno.co.uk
or by sending a cheque to Honno.
Free p&p to all UK addresses